Rode Hard

Book 1 Cowboy Code Series

Lauren Fraser

Blurb

Kat MaCray's six-week assignment on the ranch of Justin Shaw should be easy. She'll write about his rodeo career and life on the ranch and
hopefully launch herself into a well-deserved promotion.

But one look at Justin and she realizes there may be more to this trip than just work. Justin is one of the hottest cowboys around, and
he's more than happy to help Kat make the most of her time on the ranch. With his rodeo career in full swing, Justin and his friends know how to work hard
and play even harder. And Kat needs to learn how to relax and enjoy life.

Kat's walk on the wild side is only temporary—Arizona is a lifetime away from her real life in New York. But she can't deny she's starting
to fall for Justin. That doesn't change the fact she's going

home at the end of her stay. Unless she can somehow turn six weeks into happily ever after.

Contents

Chapter One

What the hell had her boss been thinking? Kat McCray scanned the dusty rodeo grounds, looking for the woman she was supposed to meet. Through the loud speakers the banter of the announcer and the rodeo clown blared across the open air, followed by laughter. A dog barked. The sound set off several others, only adding to Kat's feeling of confusion. She was a long way from New York City.

Taking a deep breath, she squared her shoulders. She could handle this. A sporting event was a sporting event. She'd done her research, watched countless hours of PRCA on TV, knew all the ins and outs of scoring. She was as ready as she was ever going to be. Unfortunately, she just hadn't quite been prepared for how chaotic everything seemed. Everyone just mixed together, contestants roamed around chatting with friends and fans. People were scattered everywhere, dogs mingled in with their owners as the cowboys congregated. How the hell was she supposed to find anyone?

Her sight rested on a group of young women. None of those women were her host. Their tight tops, short skirts and even shorter shorts looked more like they were heading out for a night on the town rather than sitting at a dusty rodeo watching men wrestle cattle to the ground.

She glanced down at her own jean-clad legs and felt decidedly overdressed. Wiggling her toes in her new boots, Kat wrinkled her nose at the layer of dust covering the formerly pristine leather. Well, if nothing else came out of this, she at least had a new pair of kickass Lucchese to wear. The cognac ostrich boots were quite possibly one of the best purchases she'd ever made. After much discussion, her boss had finally relented and let her submit the receipt for expenses. If she was going to be spending six weeks on a working ranch, the least the magazine could do was fork out for some new duds—it's not as if she could wear her Jimmy Choos on a ranch.

She lifted her long blonde hair off her neck, praying for a breeze to cool her down. Holy crap, it was hot. No wonder all the women were barely dressed. Her antiperspirant better live up to its claims because there was nothing attractive about sweat stains.

Scanning the crowd again, she spotted a tall woman with a long, chocolate-brown braid, which hung over her shoulder almost to her waist. The woman glanced over at a group of giggling girls and even from twenty feet away, Kat could see her rolling her eyes. This woman was no groupie but an honest-to-god cowgirl. Clad in a tank top and jeans, the worn boots spoke of a woman who wore them for work rather than show, despite the strip of pink leather. Kat smiled at the flash of color. That had to be her girl. Kat strolled over to the attractive brunette. "Denise?"

The woman smiled down at her. At five foot six, Kat wasn't particularly short, but next to this woman, she felt almost petite.

"You bet. You must be Kat," Denise said as she stuck out her arm. Warm, work-roughed hands encompassed Kat's palm in a firm grip.

"I am. You fit your description perfectly."

Denise laughed and stuck out her foot. "I get teased a lot about the boots." She shrugged. "What can I say, though? Even covered in manure and smelling like a horse, I still like to feel a little girly."

Kat grinned. "I don't blame you."

"So, is this your first rodeo?" Denise asked.

"That obvious, huh?"

Denise looked her over. "A little, yeah."

Great, just what she wanted—to look like a complete idiot. She wrinkled her nose and looked back at the woman who was supposed to take her under her wing for the next six weeks.

Denise and her brother owned a small working ranch and training facility just outside of Tucson. Even though he barely competed anymore, her brother Justin was one of the most recognized cowboys on the circuit, and Denise had carved out an amazing reputation for training cutting horses. The pair would make the perfect story for the sports magazine where Kat worked. Over the next several weeks, Kat was going to learn all the ins and outs of life on a ranch. Since many of the magazine's readers dreamed of life on the open trail, she was going to give them a firsthand look. The fact she might be able to give the readers a sneak peek at the life of a rodeo star was an added bonus.

"So you still game to stick around and watch some of the action?" Denise asked.

"Absolutely," Kat replied. Flapping the front of her shirt to cool herself off, Kat glanced around. Maybe she could sneak off and slip into something cooler. When she'd left home this morning it had been raining and cool, but here in Tucson it had to be close to a hundred degrees.

"Do you want a tank top or something?" Denise asked.

"Oh my god yes," Kat sighed.

"Come on, I'll get you sorted out. I always keep a few things in my brother's trailer." Denise eyed her up again and grimaced. "Sorry, it's not going to be what you're used to."

"Whatever you have will be fantastic." Kat wiped the sweat off her brow. "Is it always this hot?"

"Honey, we haven't even started to get hot yet."

"Great," Kat muttered.

Denise led her past a few sites before finally stopping in front of a large trailer with several horses tied up outside. Denise pushed open the door of the trailer and Kat followed her inside.

"You want coffee or anything to drink?" Denise asked.

"No, I'm good." Kat scanned the little kitchen area, empty water bottles rested along the edge of the sink, a couple of dirty dishes sat stacked neatly beside them, taking up the rest of the tiny counter space. Dusty jeans lay draped across the back of one chair, on another lay a pair of chaps and two pairs of worn gloves rested on the table. It was actually surprisingly clean, considering. Having been in numerous locker rooms and athletes' hotels over the years for work, Kat had expected to see more of a mess. Single guys living out of their bags tended to be notoriously untidy.

Denise rooted through a drawer under the banquet seat and pulled out a teal tank top and tossed it at Kat.

"Thanks."

"You can change in the bedroom."

Sliding the door shut behind her, Kat stripped off her shirt and slipped the tank over her head. Despite Denise's towering height, Kat was larger in one key area that made the borrowed shirt a tad uncomfortable. The ribbed knit pulled tightly across her chest, and she tugged on the arm holes to loosen the material. It was snug but a hell of a lot better than what she'd had on.

She pushed open the door and stepped out. Denise winced and started to laugh. Kat glanced down at her ample chest. "Does it look that bad?"

"No, not at all." Denise shook her head. "That shirt just looks a lot different on you than it does on me," she said and pointed to her small chest.

Kat pulled the neckline up to try to cover her cleavage. "Guess I'll fit in perfectly around here now."

Denise snorted. "Well, let's hope not. You might look like a buckle bunny but that doesn't mean you have to act like one."

"A buckle bunny?"

"Oh, come on, you're a sports writer, you know how it is with groupies. They're like the rodeo version of a puck bunny."

"Ahh got ya. Yeah, I definitely won't be acting like a buckle bunny then." Kat laughed. She'd grown up around professional athletes and they'd lost some of their mystique over the years. In her experience, the more successful the man, the bigger the ego and that was so not her thing.

She adjusted the top again. "All right, let's hit it."

Following Denise out of the trailer, Kat surveyed the grounds. The scantily clad women made so much more sense to her now. For some reason, she hadn't expected to see groupies on a rodeo circuit. At the evening dance, absolutely, but not at the dusty rodeo grounds sweating in the heat. No one could look their best after baking all day. Sweat mixing with the kicked-up dust was not a good look.

Denise led the way past the crowds and scanned the stands. A man's hand rose from the crowd and she nodded. "This way."

Kat gawked at all the fans, everyone from old, weathered cowboys to little kids sat anxiously awaiting the next event. The air hummed with anticipation. She tapped Denise on the shoulder. "What's next?"

"Bull riding." She beamed. "My brother's event."

Denise sat on the bench and nudged the person beside her to slide along. Kat dropped into the vacant seat and glanced down the line to thank the man for moving. Wow. That wasn't a man, that was a sexy Stetson commercial sitting beside Denise. The man brought his finger to the brim of his cowboy hat and smiled. His perfect teeth glistened against tanned skin.

Denise shook her head. "Don't encourage him," she told Kat.

"Huh?" Kat blinked before turning to look at the woman beside her.

"Don't encourage him. He has a big enough ego already."

The man clasped his hand to his chest. "Ouch, Dee, that hurts. How can my ego be inflated when you've been shooting me down since we were twelve?"

Denise rolled her eyes. "Right, Dunc. Kat, this is Duncan and beside him is Kasey."

Kat glanced at the two men. God, the second one was as sexy as the first. How had she missed *him?* Damn, she might become a buckle bunny yet. Wow.

Kasey tipped his hat and nodded.

"So, Kat, you must be the reporter everyone's been talking about," Duncan said.

"That's me."

He shifted on his seat to look at her. "I hear you're going to be riding out with us on Monday morning."

Kat flicked a glance between Duncan and Denise. "You work for Denise?"

"Yeah, more so now that we've cut back on traveling."

"Oh, you both compete as well?"

"Yes ma'am, but we don't do the bulls like Jus," Duncan told her.

Kat ran her eyes over Duncan. With his long, lean build, she could picture him on the back of a horse. "What events do you compete in?"

"Kase and I are partners in team, then I also do tie-down roping and he does steer wrestling."

Steer wrestling. That definitely suited Kasey's muscular build. With his wide shoulders, he looked as if he could take down a cow with ease. "You guys don't do the bulls or broncs?"

Duncan laughed. "Nah, that's for showboats like Jus."

Kat looked at Denise. "I thought your brother won all-round doing roping events?"

"He did, but since he's semi-retired, he thinks it's fun to compete in bull riding or bareback or some other such nonsense."

"Why do you call it nonsense?"

She rolled her eyes. "You'll see when it starts. I can't think of anything more stupid than getting on the back of a two-thousand-pound pissed-off bull with his nuts tied up around his throat, but that's just me." She flicked her finger toward the two men beside her. "These idiots all think it's fun."

Duncan threw up his hands. "Don't lump me in there. I like watching it, but I've never competed."

"I've seen you idiots climb on the back of a bull at the ranch after talking shit to each other, so don't give me that."

Kasey grinned, his golden-hazel eyes twinkled with amusement as he shrugged. "Come on, your brother called him a pussy, it's not like he had a choice."

"Right." Denise shook her head. "Idiots," she muttered.

Kat watched the byplay within the group with amusement. The easy friendship between the three was obvious.

The announcer's voice crackled through the PA system, announcing the first rider on the bulls. Tanner James from Texas.

Kat sat up straight, her stare focused on the chute. The gate flew open, the bull leapt free in a spin that sent the rider flying through the air and landing hard on the ground. Ouch, that had to hurt.

The second rider followed the same path as the first. The third managed to hang on a little longer but still didn't last the eight seconds. In theory, eight seconds sounded like a piece of cake, but as she watched the men being thrown off the bulls in every direction, she realized just how long eight seconds could be.

Finally, Justin Shaw's name was announced, riding Diablo's Curse. The crowd cheered in support of the hometown boy. All eyes rested on the chute, waiting for man and beast to burst free. Kat saw the rider give the nod that he was ready and the gates flew open. The bull launched into a rapid spin to the right. When he didn't shake the rider free, he bucked and snorted, sending spray flying through the air. Changing tactics, he kicked to the side. Denise's hand gripped Kat's arm tightly as they watched. Finally, after what seemed like minutes, the horn blew, announcing the rider had lasted the eight seconds. Justin dismounted, rolled and jumped to his feet. The crowd cheered.

A score of ninety-one flashed on the scoreboard and the stands erupted. That kind of score would almost guarantee a win.

The hands unwrapped from around Kat's forearm and she glanced down at the nail marks in her skin.

Denise grimaced. "Sorry about that. I always get a little nervous when he rides bulls."

Kat waved it off. "No problem." She didn't even know Justin and adrenaline zipped through her own body. Watching him had been exciting and somehow incredibly sexy. The way his muscles had bunched beneath his shirt, his forearms corded as he gripped the rope, the single-minded determination to conquer the beast. Damn, it made her kind of hot. She glanced over and Duncan caught her eye. He gave her a slow grin. Busted. God, she really wasn't much better than the buckle bunnies. The danger involved in bull riding added a whole other element to the rodeo, and oh yeah, she was a fan.

The next rider up managed to last the eight seconds but his score was considerably lower because his bull had barely put up any fight. The following two riders fell off at four and six seconds respectively.

Finally, the event was finished and Justin was announced as the winner.

Denise jumped up and grabbed Kat's arm. "Come on, let's go down and talk to Justin." When Kat stood, she glanced over at Duncan and Kasey, both men were staring at her and she shivered beneath their heated scrutiny. As if he was fully aware of the effect they both had on her, Kasey winked.

Chapter Two

Kat followed Denise and the guys through the crowd as they pushed their way past the mass of women and cowboys waiting to talk to the competitors. A cowboy strutted by and tipped his hat at them. Kat took in the tight jeans and the worn Skoal mark on his back pocket. It would have made a great shot for the magazine but somehow snapping a picture of a stranger's butt just didn't seem like the best idea.

Laughing to herself, Kat continued to follow the group. An excited squeal off to her right drew her attention to a group of women. Kat glanced over at them, then followed the line to see what had snagged their attention. A long, lean cowboy was walking toward them. The man had barely taken four steps when the young miniskirt-clad girls ran past them and swarmed around the man.

Continuing to walk, Kat watched the scene unfold as the women vied for his attention. The blonde appeared to be in the lead as she pressed her breasts against the cowboy's arm, drawing his gaze downward.

Denise rolled her eyes. "That's Brody Kyle. He's in the lead for all–round this year, so he kind of draws the fans." Denise air quoted the word "fans" and Kat smirked. If the little blonde with the inflatable breasts actually knew how the points were scored, Kat would eat her shirt.

Duncan and Kasey sauntered up and pushed past the women. "Hey, Brod, good run today. That calf gave you a run for your money."

Brody shifted his shoulder as if he were loosening a knot. "No kidding, nice purse, though."

Duncan eyed the three women surrounding Brody and nodded. "Looks like it."

Brody laughed. "You guys heading to the dance tonight?"

"Probably," Kasey replied.

"What about you, Denise? You coming too?" Brody asked.

Before she could answer, an arm wrapped around Denise's shoulder. "Ah come on, Brod, you know my sister doesn't go to those things."

Kat spun to look at the new arrival. Sweet baby Jesus, the cowboys here were incredible. This guy made Duncan and Kasey look plain. Since he hadn't glanced at her yet, she allowed herself to look her fill.

A worn cowboy hat covered his head, dark-brown hair poked out beneath the brim. She scanned the body attached to the sexier-than-sin face. Long, lean legs encased in dusty jeans and even dustier boots. Her eyes lingered on the way he filled out the fly of his jeans and she gulped. Holy cow. Continuing her survey, she focused on his rolled-up sleeves and the corded forearms, arms that had flexed and moved as he'd ridden the bull. His broad chest filled out the button-down shirt and she continued to look him over. Finally, she raised her eyes to his face, and the air whooshed out of her lungs as she was held captive by the most piercing blue eyes she'd ever seen. The pictures she'd seen of him had not even come close to preparing her for the real thing. She'd thought Denise's eyes had been striking, but on a man they were *so* much better.

A slow smile spread across his face as he did some looking of his own. His eyes lingered on her breasts and her nipples beaded tightly beneath the scrutiny. *Damn, things have a mind of their own.* She fought the urge to cover her chest.

"Justin, this is Kat. She's the reporter who's going to be staying with us," Denise said, drawing his attention from Kat's body.

His smile grew as a look of pure male confidence spread across his face. "Is that right?"

Kat nodded.

"Well then, this might not be nearly as painful as I was thinking." He stepped toward Kat and stuck out his hand. His warm, calloused palm rubbed against hers and she couldn't help wondering what those rough hands would feel like against her most sensitive flesh.

"It's nice to meet you, Kat. I'm Justin."

His voice slid across her body like a caress as he held her hand just a little longer than convention dictated.

Denise snorted. "All right, Romeo, back off. Kat didn't come here to get hit on by a bunch of horny cowboys."

Justin glanced at Kat and raised an eyebrow at her in question, daring her to disagree with his sister's claim.

Right, she was here to work. She needed this paycheck to prove to her family she could stand on her own two feet. Her dad kept expecting her to come home with her tail between her legs and she'd be damned if that was going to happen. But as she glanced over at Justin again and the sexy smile on his face, she wondered if maybe a little fling while she was here might not be such a bad thing. She was a good multitasker, after all.

She let her gaze roam down his body again. Yep, hooking up with a sexy-as-sin cowboy might be just what she needed to relieve some stress. A ranch in Arizona was a million miles away from New York. No one would be any wiser if she made the most of her time away.

Justin watched her. She shrugged as if to say "who knows" and turned her attention back to Denise. Just because she planned to have sex with him didn't mean she had to make it easy.

Later that night at the dance, Justin leaned against the wall with his beer in hand, watching with amusement as Kasey and Duncan chatted up a trio of bunnies who had approached them.

Bunny one cut herself from the herd and moved closer to Justin. She twirled the end of her blonde hair directly over her breast and her hand dragged across her nipple each time she twirled, making her nipples visible through her halter-top. She leaned in close to him. "So, cowboy, did you get enough riding in today, or do you still have some energy left?"

She licked her full lips and trailed her long nails down his chest toward his belt buckle and ran her finger along the waistband of his jeans seductively.

What the fuck was wrong with him? This girl was good to go, hot as shit and for some reason he wasn't really into her. With the adrenaline flowing through him from his win today, he should be ready to fuck anything that moved. Here this hot girl was offering, and he'd rather head home to watch *SportsCenter*. Fuck, he must be getting old.

"Well, Jus, I guess I don't need to wait around to see if you need a ride home tonight, do I?" his sister asked from beside him. Why was Denise here? She usually avoided these things like the plague.

Pushing the blonde's hand away from his belt, he turned around and nearly bumped into his annoying sister. Damn woman always thought it was so funny to rib him about the bunnies. He was just about to respond to Denise when he spotted Kat.

Holy hell. Her long, blonde hair hung down over her shoulders in a sexy, tousled mess. The kind of style women did that immediately made a man think of sex. Her blue-gray eyes twinkled with amusement as she looked at him. He'd thought she looked hot in jeans and a tank top earlier today but that was nothing compared to how she looked tonight. He'd never been a big fan of cowboy boots and miniskirts until now. The brown leather boots emphasized her shapely calves and the damn skirt was so short it made her legs look as if they were a mile long. He could already imagine how good those muscular thighs would feel wrapped around his waist. His dick twitched against the fly of his jeans. Apparently, his body just needed the right partner to kick it into gear.

"Kat," he said, tipping the brim of his hat with his finger. "Glad you decided to come."

She shrugged. "Well, your sister convinced me that I didn't want to miss seeing one of these dances in person." She looked at the group around him and his friends and she smirked. "Guess she wasn't kidding."

Justin flicked a look at his sister. Her eyes twinkled with amusement and he narrowed his stare at her.

Stepping away from the wall, he ignored the pouty look the bunny gave him as he moved closer to Kat. "So, this is your first barn dance?"

Kat scanned the dance floor. "Mmm hmm."

"And? What d'ya think?"

"The band's good."

He moved closer, the smell of her perfume drifted into his nose. Damn, she even smelled good—sweet, like vanilla and spices.

"You want to dance?"

She eyed the dance floor and chewed her bottom lip. "Umm...how attached are you to your toes?"

"Fairly." He laughed. "Don't worry, they're on there pretty good, so I think they'll hold up."

"All right then, but don't say I didn't warn you."

"Consider me warned." He placed his hand at the small of her back and led her onto the dance floor.

Grabbing her left hand with his right, he pulled her close to his body and rested his other hand on her shoulder.

Kat wrinkled her brow and looked up at him. "I thought you were supposed to have your hand on my back."

"Normally, yeah, but I kind of like dancing this way." He stroked his finger down the length of her neck and her eyes dropped closed. And right there was exactly why he preferred to keep his hand here while he danced. "You can just wrap your hand around my arm."

She wove her palm around his forearm and held on. Moving to the rhythm of the music, he led her around the dance floor. She stepped on his toes for the first few minutes but then she relaxed and let him lead. A slow song started to play, and he pulled her closer. Kat melted against him.

She felt good in his arms. All soft and curvy like a woman should be. Her full breasts pressed against his chest and he ran his hand down her back, enjoying the way she shifted against him.

Her palm ran across his arm, tracing the line from his forearm to his biceps with her fingers.

He leaned in close and let his breath blow out slowly against her ear. When she shivered, he grinned and whispered, "You want to get out of here?"

She rested her head against his shoulder and took a deep breath, then pulled back and looked him in the eye. Her eyes darkened with arousal. "I don't think that's such a good idea."

"Why not?"

Kat licked her bottom lip and he followed the path of her tongue. God, he could just imagine her running that tongue up his shaft. His jeans pulled tight against his cock as arousal shot through his body.

"Because I'm not some little groupie who is going to be all cool with a night of fun and nothing else. I'm going to be living in your family's back pocket for the next six weeks. The last thing I need to do is screw that all up by making things uncomfortable."

"Who says things would get uncomfortable?" He trailed his finger along the shell of her ear and her eyes drifted shut again. She was incredibly sensual, the way her body curled into his touch as if she couldn't get close enough. Would she be that responsive about everything? He sure as hell wanted to find out.

"Come on, Justin, look at you." She rolled her eyes. "You are totally a love 'em and leave 'em kind of guy. Everything about you screams temporary when it comes to women."

"And?"

Kat snorted. "And...what do you mean *and*? Doesn't that pretty much explain things?"

"I don't know." He let his stare roam across her face, and down, lingering on her breasts. The damn things made his mouth water. There was no way he wasn't taking her home with him tonight. He looked back at her face. "Seems to me you're only here temporarily and I don't really think I'm gonna get my fill of you in one night so—"

"So?" She raised her eyebrow at him as if she needed it all spelled out. He groaned. Typical woman, she wanted to talk things to death first.

"So, as temporary as it might be, what do you say we just enjoy ourselves while you're here?" He pulled her closer against him, allowing her to feel his erection through his jeans.

She rubbed her hips against him and smiled.

"All right, let's get out of here," he said.

She looked around, her gaze lingering on a group of scantily clad women on the edge of the dance floor. Her nose wrinkled and she shook her head. "I don't know. Let's just not rush things, okay?"

He took a deep breath and widened his stance to ease his discomfort. "No problem. But umm...if we aren't heading out, then—" He shifted again. "I need to take a little break from dancing." *Before I split my jeans open.*

Kat giggled, then slapped her hand over her mouth. "Sorry." She clamped her lips together tightly, her eyes twinkling as she tried to contain her amusement. "Let's go get a drink," she told him, still smiling.

Placing his hand at the small of her back, he led Kat off the dance floor and over toward the bar in the back corner. "What can I get you?"

"Just a beer would be good."

"Really? I'm sure they have coolers or something, if you'd prefer."

Kat snorted. "No, beer's good."

"Sorry, I just totally offended you, didn't I?"

"Little bit." She laughed. "I work for a sports magazine, Justin. You can't work in that environment and not be a beer drinker."

"Fair enough. I'll be right back."

Pushing his way through the crowd, he leaned his arms on the bar to wait his turn. A hip bumped him, and he glanced over at the little brunette beside him.

"Hi, Justin."

Crap, what was her name again? "Hey."

"It's Lisa," she said, pointing to her chest.

"Lisa, right? How's it going?" He looked back at the bartender, praying the man would come over soon.

"Much better now that I know you're here." She sidled up closer to him and brushed her breasts against his arm.

Where the hell was the bartender?

"You had a great ride today." Lisa leaned her body weight into him and stumbled, forcing him to grab her hip to hold her upright.

"You want to buy me a drink?" she asked.

He glanced over his shoulder toward Kat. She stood watching him with a mocking smile. *Damn.*

He looked down at Lisa. She was hot enough. The kind of woman he normally took home from one of these things. Hell, he already had taken her home once. He shifted uncomfortably. Even if he wasn't hoping for things to happen with Kat he'd shoot Lisa down. He never did repeats with groupies. It always gave them the wrong impression and the last thing he wanted was someone dogging him everywhere he went.

"Sorry, Lisa, I'm with someone tonight." He smiled to soften the blow.

She glanced over his shoulder toward Kat, then ran her hand along his chest. "Well, if you change your mind, come find me," she purred.

He shook his head. Here he had this woman throwing herself at him and damn if the woman he really wanted wasn't trying to brush him off. A normal guy would take the sure thing, but then he never had liked to do things the easy way.

After paying for the two beers, he wove his way through the crowd to where Kat stood waiting for him.

"Thanks for the beer. Is this where you tell me you got a better offer?" Kat nodded her head toward his right.

"What?"

He followed her direction and saw Lisa standing with her hands on her hips. The other woman stood with her friends, all watching him as if he were the prize-winning cow at the state fair.

"Not interested." He stepped closer to her. "If I'm going home with anyone tonight, sugar, it's gonna be you."

Kat took a sip of her beer. Her eyes kept flashing back to the group of women. "You sure? They seem pretty determined."

He moved toward her and she stepped back. Crowding her until her back hit the wall, forcing her to stop. With the beer bottle in his hand, he placed his knuckles on either side of her head on the wall, hemming her in. Her eyes turned a smoky gray and she licked her lips.

"I can be pretty determined when I want to be, too."

"I can see that." Her hand shook as she brought the bottle to her mouth and took a sip. He smiled. She looked around the room, pretending nonchalance, but was betrayed by a telltale tremor. It had been a long time since he'd met a woman who obviously wanted him but wasn't ready to jump into bed right away.

"Looks like your friends are leaving," she murmured.

Duncan and Kasey had a petite brunette sandwiched between them as they headed toward the exit.

"How come they're both leaving when only one of them picked up a lady?" Her brow wrinkled with a cute frown.

Justin couldn't help but laugh. He looked at Kat and raised one eyebrow in question.

She gasped. "Seriously, they're both going to sleep with her?"

"I don't imagine there'll be much sleeping, darlin'." He chuckled.

Kat blushed as she continued to stare at the three people weaving their way outside. "Do they do that a lot?"

He shrugged. "Guess it depends on your definition of a lot."

"Wow. I thought that kind of thing only happened with strippers and porn stars."

Justin burst out laughing. "Umm, nope."

Her mouth dropped open. "Do you have them too?"

He laughed at her shocked tone and tried to cover it with a cough. "Umm...well, I've been known to have tried it a time or two."

"Seriously?" Her eyes widened.

It really wasn't as big a deal as she was making it out to be. He shrugged.

"Wow, umm...so is it everything I've heard it is?" Her face flushed again but her breath hitched as she waited for his answer. Seemed his little house guest had a bit of a hidden wild side. She might not be an easy lay but she definitely would be worth the effort.

He leaned down to whisper in her ear. "With the right people it can be hotter than hell. Is that something you want to explore while you're here, city girl?"

She gasped. "Umm, yeah, no, I'm uh..." she stammered.

Justin laughed. "If you change your mind, just let me know." He nipped her ear and she groaned. "But for tonight, I want you all to myself. I've got some fantasies of my own brewing about you."

"Is that right?"

"Oh honey, that's definitely right." He ran his tongue along the shell of her ear, then sucked the lobe inside his mouth and flicked it, playing with her dangling earring with his tongue. Kat's head dropped back against the wall and her eyes closed.

He nipped the soft little spot behind her ear and she moaned.

Kat gripped the front of his shirt with her hand. "All right, cowboy, you win. Let's get out of here," she said, pushing him backward and propelling herself off the wall.

"Finally," he growled.

Chapter Three

Justin could barely keep his hands off her as they made their way to the truck. He opened her door and held it. Instead of sliding into the vehicle like he'd expected, Kat pressed her body against his. He could feel her breath against his lips when she whispered, "Drive fast."

He groaned as she pulled away and slid onto the seat. Her skirt eased up her thighs, barely covering the top of her panties. *Day-um.* He couldn't wait to feel those long legs of hers wrapped around him.

His dick was rock hard already. By the time they actually made it home, he'd be drilling through his jeans. He adjusted himself and eased into the driver's seat.

The hemi engine roared to life and he threw the truck into reverse. Gravel spewed as he ripped out of the parking lot. Kat chuckled beside him and he winced. *Yeah, real cool, Jus.* What was wrong with him? He was acting as if he was fifteen, about to get his first BJ or something. He glanced over at Kat, his eyes lingered on the bottom of her skirt. She hadn't adjusted the hem of the fabric, so it still rode precariously high on her smooth thighs. Lord have mercy. It was all he could do not to drool at the sight. He was in deep shit.

She shifted in her seat and the material slid higher. He flicked a glance at her face and she smiled. Clearly, she knew exactly what she was doing to him. Well fine, two could play at that game. Putting his eyes back on the road, he placed his hand on her knee. Heat radiated across his palm. He slid his fingers back and forth across her skin. Her legs moved apart ever so slightly to allow him to move more comfortably. He slowly glided his hand a little farther, gently caressing up and down her thigh. Her legs dropped open wider and he grinned to himself. Damn right, she wanted this as much as he did. She might play the teasing vamp but she was just as hot for him as he was for her.

Without taking his eyes off the road, he cupped her knee then slowly trailed his fingers up her thigh, dipping beneath the hem of her skirt. Kat squirmed on the seat, moving closer to his touch. He could feel the heat coming off her against his hand. On the next swipe, he dipped closer to her core, brushing his knuckles against her panties. They were already damp.

He gripped the steering wheel hard with his left hand and shifted his hips to ease the painful tightness in his jeans. Continuing to brush the back of his hand over her panties, he glanced over at Kat. Her head had dropped back against the seat, her eyes closed as her breath came more rapidly. Screw it. As much as he'd planned to just tease her, he wanted more. He wanted to see her come.

He eased beneath the fabric of her panties. His fingers slid against her smooth skin. God, she was completely bare. His cock throbbed painfully at the discovery. With no hair to infringe upon his exploration, her moisture coated his fingers and he groaned. He couldn't wait to see her laid out naked before him.

Shit, he needed to get home. Fast. He hit the gas.

Unable to resist the temptation, he swirled his finger against her clit and Kat widened her legs, allowing him full access. Sliding through her lips, he inserted his finger inside her and Kat arched off the seat. She threw her head back seductively. Her nipples poked out visibly through her shirt. Moving his finger in and out, he rubbed her clit with the heel of his hand. Kat's hips bucked in time with him, meeting him stroke for stroke. Her breath hitched and she started making the sexiest little moans.

Justin could see his house around the next corner. Almost there. He increased his tempo. He wanted her screaming her release by the time he pulled up to his house. He pressed harder against her clit as he fucked her with his finger. Kat gripped his forearm, her nails dug into his skin as her inner muscles clamped down around his finger.

"Oh god, I'm so close, Justin," she moaned.

He curled his finger slightly and she made a high-pitched groan. The sound grabbed his dick and pulled as if it was attached to a chain and he just about lost it.

"Oh yeah, right there, right there," she moaned. Her hips bucked faster and she clamped her legs together, holding his hand against her. He flicked his wrist and she screamed out her release, her muscles held his finger in place, not letting him pull out. It was going to feel like heaven when she was wrapped around his cock.

Finally, she sighed and her legs dropped open. He glanced over. Her head tilted toward him from its relaxed position against the headrest, her eyes were drowsy and the sexiest smile curled up the corners of her full lips. "Mmm, now that certainly makes the drive more fun."

He eased his hand from between her thighs and brought his fingers to his lips. He inhaled deeply, breathing in her scent. "Absolutely," he murmured, then sucked his fingers into his mouth. He groaned as his first taste of her slid over his tongue. Spicy and rich. He licked his fingers clean. He could feel her watching him, filling the truck with need. Still sucking his fingers, he looked over at her. No longer satiated and sleepy, Kat was alert and aroused. Her nipples beaded tight against her shirt, her mouth was open as she breathed rapidly. Hunger written across every inch of her body.

He flicked on the blinker and turned the truck onto the long driveway that would lead to his house. As he pulled up in front of the sprawling rancher, he threw the truck in park, grabbed his keys from the ignition and jumped out in record speed. By the time he rounded the car and opened her door, Kat had barely flicked open her seat belt. She spun on her seat and set her feet on the running board. Before she had a chance to move, he placed his hands on her thighs and slowly slid them up her legs, shoving her skirt up as he carefully pulled her toward him. Her skirt rode high around her waist. Her bright-pink bikini panties looked like something out of a lingerie catalog, the delicate lace fabric barely concealed a thing.

He gripped her hips with both hands and pulled her out of the truck. She went willingly, wrapping her legs around his waist. Her ass was tight and muscular beneath his fingers. He took a step with her wrapped around him and slammed the door shut with his foot.

Kat wove her hands around his neck and she pulled herself tighter against his body, rubbing against his erection.

"If you don't want to be fucked right here against the truck, you need to stop that," he growled.

She shivered and licked her lips as she looked at him. He grinned. Kat liked the idea of him taking her here. This was just getting better and better. He started to back her against the vehicle, but for some reason, she stopped grinding against him. Standing still, he looked at her.

She glanced around the yard as if she were looking to see if anyone was around. Her stare landed on the lights shining around the barn and she frowned. "Maybe we should go inside."

He pulled her tighter against him. "No problem." Justin walked across the yard with Kat's long, muscular legs still wrapped around his waist. His dick throbbed painfully behind the button-fly of his jeans. Each step rubbed her body against him. It was only about ten yards to the front door, but it may as well have been a mile. Need raged hard inside him.

In order to take the edge off just a little, he ran his tongue along the exposed line of her neck. Kat's head dropped to the side, giving him better access. He could taste the salt on her skin from dancing. Groaning, he nipped her earlobe between his teeth and her thighs clamped tighter around his waist.

Fuck. He gritted his teeth as he eyed the four little steps that led onto the deck. So close yet so far away. His dick dug painfully into his jeans, demanding he hurry the fuck up. Exhaling audibly, he shifted her in his arms and hit the stairs.

The moment he stepped inside, he kicked the door closed with his foot and braced her back against the door. He needed to taste her. Now. He couldn't wait. He pressed his lips against hers. Kat immediately opened for him, as hungry for contact as he was. The kiss consumed them both. Their tongues battled, devouring each other. She sucked his tongue into her mouth. With a groan, he squeezed her ass firmly in his hands.

Fingers tangled in his hair, knocking his cowboy hat onto the floor. He pushed her shirt up and whipped it over her head and dropped it on the floor beside his hat.

"Bed," she gasped, then pulled his lips back down against hers.

Justin stumbled down the hallway, bypassing his door and continuing on to the guest room where Kat would sleep. Closing the door behind him, he set her down next to the foot of the bed. God, she was gorgeous. Her eyes sparkled, the sexy tousled look she had earlier now looked like full-blown sex hair. He wanted to ride her hard from behind, bury his fingers in it and hold on.

He stood back, watching her as she shimmied out of the denim mini. It slid to the floor, leaving her standing in those sexy pink lacy panties and a matching bra. The barely there lace did even less to cover her nipples.

They beaded tightly against the fabric, clearly visible against the lace. The pink lace tormented him, making him wonder what color her nipples were. "Lose the bra," he demanded.

Kat's eyes darkened as she watched him. Never breaking eye contact, she slowly reached behind her back and released the clasp. The bra slid down her arms and she held the fabric against her chest, a smile curved up the edges of her mouth.

Jesus. His throat felt as if he'd been branding horses for two days. So dry and gritty he couldn't even swallow. He was practically on his tiptoes, trying to peek as she teasingly lowered her hands so he could just see the tip of her nipples.

"Pink," he muttered.

"What?" she asked.

"Nothing." He gripped her hips but held her at arms' length. "Drop your hands," he ordered.

She lowered her palms and the bra fluttered to the floor, giving him his first full view of her breasts. He groaned. She looked even better than he'd imagined. He wrapped his arms around her waist and pulled her flush against him, grinding his hips into her, letting her feel how turned-on he was. Justin bent and sucked one ripe berry into his mouth, swirling his tongue around it. He backed her up until he felt her legs hit the edge of the mattress.

Kat broke the kiss and sat on the edge of the bed. She looked at him and smiled. When he moved toward her, she held up her hand. "Hang on, cowboy, I want to get a look at the goods, too."

"Oh, is that right?"

"Mmm hmm, I keep hearing about these rock-hard abs that all you cowboys have, so I think I need to make sure you live up to the hype." She twirled her finger through her long hair as she grinned at him, trailing the lock across her breast. Her nipple hardened. The gesture was the same as the bunny earlier but somehow when Kat did it, it was so much hotter.

Even though it was only her eyes running over him, his body reacted as if she'd touched him and his dick twitched beneath her stare. He dropped into the chair in the corner and pulled off his boots. Times like these, he wished he was the kind of guy to wear something besides boots. The things were a pain in the ass to get off when you were rock hard.

Finally, both boots lay on the floor beside him. He stood and slowly walked toward the bed. He undid the top button of his shirt, then the next. Kat tracked the movement of his fingers. Her tongue dipped out when he undid the third, then fourth buttons. He could get undressed faster but he had to admit he was really enjoying how turned-on she got from watching him. He pulled the fabric out of his jeans and undid the last two buttons. As he started to lower the shirt from his shoulders, Kat gasped.

"Wow, they weren't lying," she sighed. Standing, she moved toward him.

His eyes never left hers as he dropped the shirt on the floor. Kat trailed her fingers along the ridges between his muscles. What was it with women and his abs? They all seemed to be amazed by them.

The feel of her delicate, reverent touch made his muscles constrict. Her eyes widened. "I thought they called it a six-pack but this...this is an eight-pack. I didn't even know that was possible."

He shrugged.

"Oh honey, there's no need for modesty. Hell, if I had my way you'd walk around shirtless the entire time I was here."

He grinned. "I will if you will."

She pretended to scowl. "So not the same thing."

"You're right, yours are much better. But I don't imagine the guys would get much work done if they got to look at you all day."

She sucked in a breath and her nipples looked like pebbles.

"You like the idea of the guys looking at you?" he murmured and swept his finger over her nipple.

"What? No," she scoffed.

"Hmm, maybe you just like the idea of a couple of the guys looking at you." He swept his tongue around the swollen bud. "Maybe Kasey or Dunc?"

She moaned.

"Or maybe both of them?"

She squeezed her thighs together. Oh yeah, she definitely liked that idea. Well, he could arrange that, but for tonight she was all his. And he planned to enjoy every minute of it.

Justin hooked his fingers into the waistband of her panties and eased them down her thighs. With her completely naked, he swept her into his arms and laid her on the bed, her blonde hair fanned out across the pillow. Holy hell. His cock throbbed.

She was incredible. Looking down at her, he flicked open his belt and ripped open the buttons on his jeans.

He pushed down his jeans and underwear together in one fell swoop.

"Well, hello," Kat murmured, a smile on her lips as she stared at his erect cock.

He stepped out of his jeans and eased himself onto the bed, coming down on top of her. Kat opened her legs, making room for him. "Hang on one second," he said. Justin reached over and pulled the condom from his wallet and set it on the pillow, then dropped the wallet and jeans back onto the floor.

"Now where was I?" he whispered. "Oh yeah, I remember."

He brushed a kiss against her lips. What started out as a slow, soft kiss quickly morphed into something much more carnal and hungry. Their tongues tangled and his hips moved of their own volition. Her hot, wet pussy rubbed against his cock and he groaned. Man, he wanted to bury himself in her right now but then the anticipation would be over already and he planned to take his time with her. Foreplay, the hunger and yearning, was the best part of the hunt. There was nothing he liked more than making a woman squirm with need, and something about Kat made the desire stronger. He wanted her panting, begging for him. Seeing her come in the truck had given him a hint of what she looked like in the throes of passion and he really wanted to see her completely undone. *Before he was.*

He broke the kiss and ran his tongue down her neck, across the top of her breast. Goose bumps pooled on her skin from the touch. *Nice.*

He swirled his tongue around her right nipple and her legs dropped open against the mattress.

Moving over, he sucked the other bud into his mouth and flicked the right one with his fingers, twisting slightly between his fingertips. Kat moaned and arched her back, pressing herself closer to him. Damn, the woman was so incredibly sensual.

Teasingly kissing his way down her body, he dipped his tongue into her bellybutton then continued lower, positioning himself between her legs. Inhaling deeply, musky arousal filled his senses and he groaned. "I didn't get nearly a good enough taste of you earlier."

She smiled and widened her legs. "Well then, by all means, enjoy."

Justin growled. Fuck, there was nothing sexier than a confident woman in bed. He spread her lips apart with his fingers. Flattening his tongue, he made one long, slow swipe of her pussy. Now that's what he was talking about. He swirled his tongue around her clit and, using her movements as a guide, went firmer and softer with his tongue. He sucked the hard nub into his mouth and she bucked off the bed.

"Oh my god, Justin," she moaned.

He bit back a grin. Guess she liked that. He inserted his finger inside her and she rocked her hips against his face. Her fingers laced into his hair and she held him against her body. She had him clamped so tightly, there was no way she was letting him go anywhere until he was done, which was fine by him because this was exactly where he wanted to be. He fucked her harder with his finger, matching her rhythm while he continually flicked her clit with his tongue.

"Oh god, that feels good," she sighed.

"Mmm," he hummed against her, enjoying the way she shivered beneath his mouth. Her fingers dug into his scalp almost painfully as she rocked against him. Her thighs tightened around his ears, practically smothering him. Oh yeah, she was close. Lust surged through him. He inhaled deeply, trying to remain in control of his body as the need to bury himself in her threatened to take over. Kat's musky arousal filled his senses, making him growl. Slurping her clit into his mouth again, he curled his finger inside her and she screamed out her release. Her legs clamped around him like a vise as she rode out her orgasm.

Finally, her legs eased and flopped down onto the mattress, her fingers uncurled from his hair and she released him. Sitting back on his knees, he put his fingers in his mouth and groaned. He looked down at her. "That was hot."

"That's putting it mildly," she said. Her eyes were half closed and slumberous, her skin flushed with arousal. "So, how do you want me?" she asked.

Justin gulped. No woman had ever asked him that before, and certainly not with a look on her face that said she'd be up for anything he threw at her. The picture from earlier of her on her knees with him pulling her long hair flashed through his mind and his cock throbbed painfully. He cleared his throat. "From behind work for you?"

A slow, sexy smile spread across her lips. "Oh from behind definitely works for me."

She rolled over and pushed her ass into the air, moving from side to side as she got up on her knees. Justin groaned. He was going to enjoy having her here for the

next few weeks. No commitment, just pure unadulterat-
ed smoking-hot sex.

He grabbed the condom, ripped into the package and
sheathed his cock. Placing himself at the entrance to her
pussy, he paused. Kat glanced at him over her shoulder,
smiled and pressed back. That was all the invitation he
needed. He gripped her hips with his hands and pushed
forward. She was so wet he slid right inside. With a grunt,
he drove into her, burying himself balls-deep.

They both groaned.

He wrapped his hand in her long hair and gently pulled
her head back. Her hot, tight pussy clenched around
him, her body letting him know she liked playing a little
rough. He eased back slowly, then thrust back deep.
Continuing his rhythm, he drove them both higher. His
balls pulled up tightly, his orgasm was close. He reached
around her and flicked her clit with his other hand.

Kat arched her back like a cat, throwing her head
back, and he held on tighter as he pounded into her.
The deeper he went, the louder she moaned in pleasure.
The sound of his balls slapping against her ass fueled him
on. He rode her hard, loving how into it she was as she
pressed back against him, driving him deeper with each
thrust. He rubbed her hardened nub with his fingers. She
groaned out her release as her pussy clenched around
him, milking his cock. That was all he needed to send
him over the edge.

His balls drew up tight as heat shot down his spine and
along his shaft as he came. The orgasm that tore through
him nearly knocked him on his ass with its intensity. His
arm shook as he fought to hold his weight off her rather

than collapsing onto her back like his body wanted him to.

He untangled his hand from her hair and she dropped her head down. Her loud breathing matched his own as they both gasped. Resting against her back, he placed a kiss between her shoulder blades and she shivered. He ran his tongue up her back and nipped the soft skin at the nape of her neck and her pussy clenched tightly around his cock. He'd have to remember that spot for next time. He carefully pulled out of her and disposed of the condom in the wastebasket beside the bed. Kat collapsed onto the mattress on her stomach, her face buried in the pillow.

Dropping down beside her, he ran his hand down her spine and rested his palm on her butt. She had a fantastic ass. After several minutes, Kat turned her head and looked at him. "Now I know where the saying 'rode hard and put away wet' comes from."

He burst out laughing. That was quite possibly the last thing he'd expected her to say.

She rolled onto her side and smiled. "That was amazing. Holy shit. Wow, we are so doing that again as soon as possible. I just need a minute." She closed her eyes and sighed. When she opened them again, her eyes were twinkling with mischief. "But next time I'm on top. I have to try out that whole 'save a horse ride a cowboy thing' if that's all right with you."

"You've been listening to too much country music." He laughed. He rolled onto his back and placed his hands behind his head. Damn, he felt good. He sighed. "Honey, you can ride me anytime you want."

She glanced down his body and her eyes widened when they landed on his cock as it sprang to life again. "Already? Mmm, there is something to be said for clean living."

"We're just getting started showing you all the benefits to life on a ranch," he said. Cupping the back of her head, he pulled her in to a kiss. He intended to show her exactly how amazing things could be while she was here.

Chapter Four

The sun poked its way through her sleep-filled haze. Peeking open her eyes, she glanced at the bedside clock. Seven-eighteen. Way too early to wake up on a Sunday morning. Kat rolled over and glanced at the empty space beside her. Instinctively, she'd known Justin wasn't the type to wait around for the awkward morning-after discussion. Hell, she'd known when he'd carried her to her room that he was keeping things nice and casual. But still, that didn't stop the stab of disappointment that cut through her gut.

Kat rolled out of bed and quickly dressed. She slid on a pair of jeans, tank top and boots before slathering sunscreen on every inch of exposed flesh. With one last look in the mirror, Kat inhaled deeply and opened her bedroom door. From down the hall, she could dimly hear the clinking of glass and soft chatter. Following the sound, she strolled into the kitchen.

The sight seemed so normal, like a real family, not that she'd ever experienced that firsthand, but it was just what she'd always pictured a family looking like.

Denise stood with her back to Kat at the large gas range, spatula in hand as she tended to several frying pans all loaded up with various breakfast fare.

"Good morning, Kat," Duncan said, watching her from his place at the table.

Denise spun around. "Oh Kat, morning. Sorry, I didn't know you were up. Let me get you some coffee."

Waving her off, Kat smiled. "You're busy enough without waiting on me. Just point me in the direction of the cups and I'll help myself."

Kasey hopped up from the table, opened the oak cabinet beside the fridge and handed her a heavy stoneware mug.

"Thanks," she murmured. Pouring herself a cup of coffee, she liberally added creamer until it looked the right color and scooped in a spoonful of sugar. Kat brought the cup up to her lips and inhaled deeply. "Mmm." Now that was exactly what she needed to kick her body into gear. The first sip of the steamy brew was like liquid heaven. Every cell in her body sighed with pleasure as the caffeine zipped through her system.

Coffee in hand, Kat eased herself into a vacant seat at the table. She couldn't help wondering where Justin was. Judging by the spread of food Denise was cooking up, she expected more than just the four of them for breakfast. Her stomach clenched as she anticipated seeing him again. Would things be awkward if he pretended nothing had happened between them or would Justin treat her like a woman he was interested in? Damn it, they should have discussed this last night.

"Kat?"

She glanced up to find Denise, Kasey and Duncan all staring at her. Oh crap, how long had she been zoned out in her own little world?

"Sorry, I missed that," she apologized.

"No problem, I just asked how hungry you were?"

No sooner had the question been asked than her stomach rumbled loudly.

"I guess you're hungry." Denise laughed, then loaded up dishes with eggs, hash browns, bacon and pancakes and set them on the table, then took her own seat.

Kat's eyes widened as she stared at the spread placed on the table before her. Good lord, if she ate like this every morning, she'd never fit into any of her clothes back home. For her, a normal breakfast consisted of a cup of coffee and a piece of toast or maybe a banana.

Watching Kasey and Duncan pile up their plates with food, she stared in awe. No way they'd be able to eat all that. Would they? Kasey rolled up a pancake and shoved half of it into his mouth with his fingers. As he lowered his hand, Denise whacked it with her fork. "Hey, come on, manners, Kase."

He glanced at Kat and mumbled, "Sorry," around his mouthful of pancakes.

"No problem." She stared in awe as they all continued to fill their plates.

"I thought you were hungry," Denise said.

"I am." She placed two pancakes and two strips of bacon on her plate.

"Is that all you plan to eat?" Duncan asked her.

"Mmm hmm."

"You're gonna need to eat more than that tomorrow if you're working, we don't stop until noon usually, so you'll need lots of fuel to make it."

She smiled at him. "I'll be fine."

Duncan shrugged. "All right, but don't say I didn't warn you."

"Noted."

Trying to be casual, she glanced toward the back door.

"Jus is already out working, a neighbor spotted a coyote this morning on the east pasture and gave us a call, so Justin's out dealing with it."

The tension she hadn't even realized she had in her shoulders eased. Maybe he hadn't slipped out to avoid the morning-after thing at all.

"Do you get a lot of coyotes here?" she asked no one in particular.

Duncan shrugged. "I don't know. Guess it depends on your definition. It's a big ranch and as the weather gets hotter, the animals go to ground, hiding from the heat, so food becomes scarcer. It makes the predators get a bit more daring looking for a meal. Thankfully, there are plenty of ranches around, so they seem to spread out their attacks a bit."

The phone rang, interrupting the discussion around the table. Denise answered and after a brief conversation, she hung up and sat back down. "That was Jus. He's on his way back in. He said to ask you to meet him at the barn and he'd take you out and show you a bit of the ranch, so you were ready to dig in tomorrow."

Eager to see Justin again, she shoveled her food into her mouth and gulped down the last of her coffee.

Denise laughed. "No need to rush. It will take Jus at least fifteen or twenty minutes to get back to the barn, so you have time."

Heat ran across her cheeks. Busted. God, could she be more obvious? She forced herself to slow down and eat the last couple of bites normally. Done, she pushed away from the table and put her plate in the dishwasher. Trying to look casual, she looked around the room.

Denise caught her eye and shook her head. "Just go." She chuckled.

Kat turned to say bye to the guys and found them watching her. Kasey's eyebrow arched in speculation, desire and interest burned in his eyes. He studied her as if trying to decide what the news meant. Duncan flashed her a bad-boy grin she couldn't even begin to interpret. If she didn't know better, she'd think finding out she was eager to see Justin had just made her more appealing to these two rugged cowboys.

"I'll see you guys at lunch then I guess," Kat said.

"You bet. Have fu-un," Denise sang.

Outside in the yard, Kat looked around at the expansive land. It seemed to go for miles and miles before meeting up with the rocky slopes of the Santa Catalinas. She couldn't even begin to imagine what it must be like to live out here. Even with the cattle milling about, it was so quiet. She could actually hear herself think. Not something she'd ever been able to say in New York. She inhaled deeply and coughed. The air was too clean. Her lungs didn't even know what to do with it. Where was the smog and car exhaust?

She rested her elbows on the top rung of the corral to wait for Justin. A cool breeze brushed against her skin and she leaned her head back to enjoy the feel of the sunshine on her face. As much as she didn't want to admit it, it was incredibly peaceful here. She could certainly understand the appeal.

After several minutes, she opened her eyes and scanned the horizon before she saw him riding across the land toward her. He looked amazing, so comfortable in the saddle. Man and beast moved as if they were one unit, each an extension of the other as they raced across the field. She'd never seen anyone ride with that kind of ease.

Her heart thumped against her chest. What would things be like when he reached her? Would there be that awkward morning-after, light-of-day discomfort? She certainly hoped not.

Justin rode up and stopped at the edge of the pen. As he dismounted, Kat strolled over and stopped beside him while he looped the reins over the rail. The beautiful buttery Palomino nickered and pushed her shoulder with his head. Kat laughed. "All right, you bossy thing." She ran her hand down the horse's soft muzzle. "Aren't you gorgeous?"

The horse nickered again, as if agreeing with her. Glancing at Justin, she asked, "What's his name?"

"Scout." Justin's deep voice slid over her body. He glanced around the yard. They were completely alone. A slow, sexy smile spread across his face as he moved closer to her. He wrapped his hand around the back of her neck and pulled her toward him, lining up their bodies.

"Morning," he whispered against her lips, then kissed her. When they parted, they were both breathing heavily. "Sorry I wasn't there this morning, I wanted to talk to you before I left, but holy smokes, woman, you are virtually impossible to wake up."

She laughed. "I know, it's awful. I sleep like the dead. I have to set three alarms every morning to make sure I hear them."

"That explains it." He looked at her and held her stare. Heat flared between them. Justin cleared his throat. "Right, well, if I plan to get any work done today, I think we should uh...get rolling."

"Sounds good."

"You ever been on a horse before?"

"Yeah, I grew up riding."

"Great, that makes things easy." As they were talking, an older gentleman walked toward them with a saddled Appaloosa. Justin looked up. "Thanks, Jimmy." The older man nodded as he stopped in front of them.

"Kat, this is Jimmy, Jimmy, Kat, she'll be staying with us for the next six weeks or so." He turned to Kat. "Jimmy has been working here since before I was born, so if you want to know anything about the area, he's the one to ask."

The grizzled old cowboy looked down at his boots and made a grumbling noise. She wasn't sure if it was one of agreement or not.

Kat ran her hand along the nap of the Appaloosa. "And what's your name?" she asked the horse.

"That's Slick, he'll be nice and gentle with you," Justin told her.

The horse nickered in agreement.

"All right then, let's get going. Do you need help getting on or are you good?" Justin asked.

Kat bristled at the implication that she needed help getting on her horse. "I'm fine, thanks."

Justin chuckled and tipped his hat at her. "All righty." He walked over to his own horse and in one smooth movement, he was atop Scout.

"Show-off," she muttered. Even with her long legs, it was a big reach to put her foot into the stirrup. With her foot situated, she grabbed the horn of the saddle and bounced, once, twice and up she went onto the horse. Adjusting herself on the saddle, she took hold of the reins in both hands and sat up tall. It would definitely take some getting used to riding on a western saddle. Finally, feeling as if she was ready, she glanced over at Justin, who watched her with a little smirk on his face.

"We good?" he asked.

"Mmm hmm."

He started the horses at an easy walk. Unfortunately, her horse kept shaking his head.

Justin stopped alongside her. "Maybe just try holding the reins looser in one hand."

She looked at him, puzzled. "Why?"

"He's not used to getting pulled like that from both sides."

Kat wrinkled her brow but did as he suggested and transferred the reins to one hand and immediately the horse calmed beneath her. Huh, guess that was the problem after all.

Justin snickered. "Sorry, he's not a fancy English kind of guy."

"Ha ha." She shifted on the saddle, trying to get her seat. Was it that obvious that she'd never ridden western? Great way to impress a cowboy by looking like a total city slicker.

Justin walked his horse over so he was practically resting against hers, with his thigh pressed up behind her leg. He placed his hand at the small of her back. "Slouch down in your seat a little."

She curled her back.

He pushed a foot against hers in the stirrup. "Turn your foot out a little." Doing as she was instructed, she moved her feet, the action forced her hips to shift deeper into the seat.

Justin nodded. "Yeah, more like that." He adjusted the cowboy hat Denise had lent her and winked. "Now you look like a cowgirl, so let's see what you've got."

Several hours later, Justin led Kat back toward the barn. He eased himself off his horse and looped the reins over the post. By the time he got over to Kat, she was easing her leg over Slick's back with painstaking care. It looked as if every one of her movements hurt. She'd no sooner planted her feet on the ground than she stumbled backward into his arms. If he hadn't been standing behind her, she would have fallen on her ass. With a groan, Kat leaned against his chest and bent her legs. "Oh my god, my knees hurt."

"It takes a little bit of getting used to." He laughed. She'd done really good considering she didn't do this every day. He rubbed her shoulders and she groaned. The raw, pleasured sound instantly shot a bolt of lust directly to his cock.

"Mmm, that feels good." Kat tilted her head forward. He dug his thumbs into the knots on her neck.

"Holy crap, you've got magic hands." Kat practically purred beneath his palms.

"Oh yeah, does that mean you don't want me to stop?"

"Want you to stop? Hell no, I'll be your frickin' slave if you don't stop."

His dick twitched against his fly. "My slave, huh?" He liked the sound of that. A picture of Kat on her knees sucking his cock flashed through his mind. He pressed his hips against her ass. "So what exactly does being my slave entail?"

She smacked his arm. "Geez, perv, not what you're thinking."

Justin chuckled. "How do you know what I'm thinking?"

"Oh I don't know, maybe the big hard dick in my ass." She snorted.

Justin groaned as the dick in question flexed at the idea of being in her ass. He pushed his hips against her and rubbed. "If my dick was in your ass, honey, you'd be moaning, not laughing."

Kat snorted again. "We'll see, cowboy."

He gripped her hips and spun her around. He wrapped his hand around the back of her neck and pulled her head toward him. He held her stare. "You can count on it, Kat," he whispered.

Chapter Five

K at sat down on the porch swing and dug into her bag for her notebook and pen while she waited for Justin to come back outside. She tipped her head back and enjoyed the feel of the early evening breeze as it blew across her cheeks. It really was incredibly beautiful here. So quiet and peaceful.

It had taken a few days to get used to the slower pace, but now she really enjoyed it. Lord knows they'd made her work full days at a backbreaking pace, but when she took lunch with the other staff, she actually took lunch. Not a working lunch at her desk, but an honest to god lunch with real conversation that didn't revolve around work. It was kind of nice.

At the sound of the screen door closing, she opened her eyes and sucked in a breath at the sight of Justin walking towards her. Mmm, the man hit every one of her buttons. She'd never met anyone like him.

Over the past couple of years working for the magazine, she'd interviewed several athletes. Unfortunately, most of the time, their egos matched their salaries. From what she'd seen of Justin, so far, that didn't seem to be the case.

He sat down on the swing beside her and handed her an ice-cold beer. Justin glanced at her notepad and wrinkled his nose. "Alright, let's get this over with."

She leaned back against the arm of the swing and pulled her leg up on the seat so she could face him more comfortably. "I promise not to make this part too painful."

Grabbing her pad and pen, she pulled the cap off and hooked it onto the back of the pen. "Most of what I want to learn I'll do just through conversation with everyone during my time here, but it'd be great to get a little bit of meat around your time on the circuit if that's cool with you."

He took a pull on his beer, then looked at her. "Sure. What do you want to know?"

"You won all-around three years in a row. That's a pretty major accomplishment."

"I got lucky. Pulled some good stock and that went along way towards my wins."

She smiled. "I think it's a little more than pulling good stock, Justin."

He shrugged. "It certainly didn't hurt."

"No, I'm sure it didn't." She took a sip of her beer as she studied him.

"You were at the top of your game when you stopped competing as seriously. Most people would have kept going, rode the high a little longer. Everyone was surprised you didn't come back guns a blazing for another victory this season and are kind of taking things a bit easy."

"It was time." He swiped a drop of condensation as it ran down the beer can and rubbed his hand on his jeans.

When he didn't say anything further, Kat sighed. Okay, maybe she needed to go at things a little differently.

"So why did you choose the events you did?"

"Honestly? Because they are fun. The payout is usually pretty good if you can place." He crossed his boot over his knee and leaned back on the swing. "I started with tie-down roping because as a rancher's son, you better know how to do that well." He smiled absently. "My first competition I just did tie-down for fun to see if I could do it and I won." He looked at her and his mouth curled up in a crooked grin. "Not gonna lie, the money was a big draw. I was sixteen and had a bunch of cash in my pocket from a weekend's work and I thought I'd died and gone to heaven."

"And did you keep thinking that?"

"Shit no." He shook his head. "I started doing bull and saddle bronc for the challenge and started winning and..." he broke off.

"And what?" she asked.

"No, nothing really. It opened up some doors and possibilities I didn't think were possible before that." He stood up and walked to the railing.

Kat watched him as he looked over his land, lost in thought, surveying his surroundings. After several minutes, he turned back around and smiled.

"Rodeo allowed me to pay off this land and for Dee and I to expand, which was really cool."

"This place is beautiful," she murmured.

"Yeah, it is." He leaned against the railing. "So what else do you want to know about rodeo life?"

"You met Kasey and Duncan while you were on the circuit?"

"No, Dunc and I have been friends forever, but I met Kasey on the circuit. Duncan's actually why I started riding bulls and broncs." He smiled to himself. "The first time I rode a bull was on a dare. We'd had a couple drinks and I was talking trash to some of the guys and Dunc dared me to put my name down and show 'em how it's done." He laughed. "Man, that bull kicked my ass, but what a rush."

"You were hooked?"

"Yeah. I was eighteen and cocky as all hell and determined to show those bulls who's boss." He glanced out at the corral and shook his head. "I broke my collarbone and a couple of ribs before I finally started to get the hang of things. There's a little more to it than just hanging on and hoping for the best."

"I gather you don't like not being good at something."

He chuckled. "Hate it. I spent every waking hour practicing and getting better at it. The transition to broncs wasn't as hard." He ran his hand through his hair and pushed it off his forehead. "Like I said, rancher's kid, breaking horses and roping cattle was par for the course. Riding bulls? Not so much."

"So no drunken bull rides as a teenager?"

Justin laughed. "Nah, I was smarter than that."

Kat looked at him and grinned. "Smart enough not to do it at home, but not smart enough not to do it when the bull is confined to a chute with his ball's tied up to his neck? I think it would have been smarter to try when he was free on the range."

"Where's the challenge in that?" He winked and said, "plus the pays a lot better."

"I'll give you that one."

A stream of cows mooing drifted across the air, and Justin turned to look back out across the land. Kat studied him. What made someone like him tick? To walk away from the fame and money of being at the top of the rodeo circuit and come home to this quiet ranch in Arizona.

"I imagine you would have given up a lot of endorsements when you eased up a bit."

"Yep," he agreed.

"Was that hard to walk away from?"

"Umm," he rubbed the back of his neck. "I'm not sure how to answer some of this stuff. It's kind of weird because you're here staying with us and it feels friendly, but at the end of the day you're writing an article as well, so I don't know what's going into the article."

"Justin, believe me, my goal is not to make anyone look bad in the least. I want to give a glimpse at life on the ranch and the glamour of being on the rodeo circuit." She leaned forward and rested both her feet on the ground. "Why don't I let you read it before I submit it to my editor? Would that make things more comfortable?"

He nodded and smiled and it was like she could see the nerves slid out of his body. "Yeah, definitely."

"Good, so did you enjoy the fame of being on tour?"

"Certain aspects of it were fun. Other's not so much." He wrinkled his nose.

"Okay, what memory were you just thinking about there?"

He winced and rubbed his neck again as a blush ran up his neck.

"Oh, now you have to tell me," she said, enjoying his discomfort.

"It's embarrassing," he mumbled.

She rested her elbows on her knees as she watched him. "I promise I won't laugh."

"Yeah, you will," he said. "Fine. Um... having fans was normally really cool. I liked when kids came up after the show and wanted to talk or get their hats signed. But sometimes the fans were a little more eager than others and that could be challenging."

The redness on his ears deepened and Kat grinned. Now she really needed to hear this story. "Like what kind of things did they do?"

He glanced at her and sighed. "You really want to hear this?"

"Yes, definitely."

"Fine, this one time I got back to my trailer and no-ticed the door wasn't quite closed all the way, which was weird, but wasn't the first time a woman had broken into my trailer." He shook his head. "Except it was the first time I found a middle-aged guy in my bed."

Kat covered her mouth as she laughed. "Oh no."

"Oh yeah, and it got worse." He laughed. "While I was trying to usher him out and explain I was flattered but not into men, his wife knocked on the door, then they proceeded to try and entice me into having a threesome with them."

She snorted as pictured the scene he was describing. "Oh my god, they did not."

"Oh, they did." He shook his head. "It was awful. It would have been fine if they had just accepted the no and left, but they kept trying to persuade me. There's really no polite way to say are you kidding? Get the hell out of my trailer."

Tears streamed down Kat's cheeks as Justin animatedly described the scenario. "That's awesome."

"Not the word I would use for it."

Kat wiped her eyes and leaned back in her seat. Their eyes met and held. With his face flushed with laughter, he was even more attractive than normal. She could see why fans tried to sneak into his trailer. She cleared her throat. *Let's try this again.* "You're competing a lot less this year, why the change in schedule?"

He strolled toward her and sat back down on the swing. "It's a hard life travelling, being away from home. In order to stay where I needed to in the standings, I had to compete enough to pull the points and it started to take a toll on my body."

"But you're still competing?" she pressed.

He chuckled. "Yeah, it's hard to walk away from it all completely." He glanced over at her. "The adrenaline of bull riding is unlike anything else, and it still calls me now and then, even though I know it shouldn't."

"Why shouldn't it?"

"Dee thinks I should just quit while I'm ahead and not press my luck and she's probably right, which is why I walked away from the main pro-circuit." He flashed her a boyish smile and she couldn't help but grin back at him. "Sometimes you just have to test yourself and know that you rode hard and hope you don't get your ass handed to you in the process."

He draped his hand across the back of the swing and twirled a piece of her hair with his fingers. "What made you want to be a sportswriter?"

"Initially, my dad." She set down her notepad and focused all of her attention on Justin. "My dad was one of those men who wanted a son, not a daughter. Growing up, the only way I could get him to spend any time with me was watching sports." She looked down at the pen in her hand as memories flooded in.

"So you liked watching sports?"

Kat chuckled. "Not at first, no. Initially, I only did it to get my dad's attention. We could go days without him saying more than couple words to me, but as soon as we sat down to watch a game, he never shut up."

Justin picked up her hand and threaded their fingers together. His palm felt so warm against hers. "Gradually, over time, I fell in love with watching sports. All the little intricacies of the various games. It was like a puzzle, trying to figure out what offence or defense worked best against each opponent." She turned his hand over on her lap and traced her fingers along the scars on his palm. He had working hands, covered in scars and callouses. Strong, competent, the hands of someone who wasn't afraid of hard work.

"Unfortunately, I was average at best at playing most sports, but that didn't stop me from loving everything about them. I loved the energy of the game." She cocked her head to the side as she studied him. "I'm sure you know what I'm talking about. The energy of the crowd in the stadium before you ride. How everyone collectively holds their breath at those key moments. It's awesome."

"Yeah, no, it's definitely addictive. That's part of why I still dabble now and then. Ridings a rush, but the crowd adds to that for sure."

Justin picked up her legs and pulled them over his lap. "So what does your dad think of you writing for a sports magazine? I bet he must think that's cool?"

That's not exactly how she'd describe what her dad thought of her job. She cringed as she thought of the last couple of conversations they'd had. How she was working in a man's world and if she wasn't tough enough to hack it, there probably were fifteen guys waiting in line who were. She shifted the pillow behind her back to get more comfortable. "He likes the free tickets I can occasionally get him."

"He's not proud of you?" He rubbed her leg gently.

"Umm. I'm sure he is in his own way. That's just not really the relationship we have. We aren't really a close family like you are."

Justin made an odd sound in the back of his throat that drew Kat's eyes. "What? You don't think your family is close?" she asked.

"No, Dee and I are really close. Our dad's just sound a lot alike."

"Really?"

"Mmm," he murmured as his hand trailed up her calf.

"Are you trying to distract me from this conversation?" she asked.

He raised his head and met her stare. "Would it work if I did?"

Kat's gaze lingered on his face and his eyes darkened. He licked his lips as he watched her. "Probably," she replied.

Justin grabbed her legs and gave a little tug, dragging her down on the swing. Kat squealed.

The screen door banged open. "Quit fondling our guest," Dee said as she came out onto the porch.

Kat giggled and pushed herself upright. "Hey. We were just finishing up some interview questions."

"Mmm hmm, is that what the kids are calling it these days?" She smirked.

"Did you need something?" Justin asked.

"The guys and I were thinking of playing poker and thought we'd see if you two wanted to play," Dee said.

Kat pushed herself upright on the swing. "Absolutely. What's the buy in?"

"Just twenty bucks and you can rebuy up to two times at twenty a pop," Dee replied.

"I'm in. I just have to grab some cash out of my room." Kat stood up and glanced at Justin.

He rolled his eyes. "Alright, I guess we're playing poker."

Chapter Six

Friday, after a long grueling day of work with Denise training cutting horses, Kat raised the brim of her hat off her forehead and dragged her sleeve along her face to wipe the grit and grime off her skin. What she needed was a nice hot shower. She bent over at the waist to stretch her back. With a groan, her hands immediately went to her aching muscles.

She couldn't believe she'd fallen off her horse today. Putting a cutter through its paces was a lot harder than it looked. When Slick had cut hard to the right to chase a calf, Kat had flown left and landed on a heap on the ground. Thank god Justin and the guys hadn't been anywhere around when she'd fallen or there would be no way they'd take her with them next week.

Kat dropped the curry comb into the bucket, untied her horse from the post and set him loose in the field. She hoisted her saddle from its spot beside Denise's on the fence. With the saddle on her shoulder, she turned to Denise. "I'll put the tack away if you want to grab first shower."

"No, leave it, I can put it away." Denise waved her hand.

"Don't be silly, you've done it all week. I'm pretty sure you've more than earned first shower after putting up with me."

Denise watched her and wrinkled her nose. "You sure?"

"Absolutely."

"That would be amazing." Denise sighed. "You did good today. I think you're really getting the hang of things. It's been a huge help having you around. I'm not sure I want you to go work with the guys for the next couple weeks."

"You never know, they might get sick of me the first day and send me packing."

Denise snorted. "Yeah right, judging by the way they all look at you I'm surprised they let you work with me this long."

"What do you mean they all look at me?"

"Oh come on, Kat, you know exactly what I mean, all three of them are like frickin' walking hard-ons the second you get near them."

"No, they're not." She grinned as she remembered the way Justin had pressed up against her in the kitchen the night before, and despite his sister and friends being in the room, he'd proceeded to whisper all the dirty details about what he planned to do to her when he got her alone. "Well, maybe your brother."

Denise rolled her eyes. "Yeah and his two cronies want to join in or watch at the very least."

"No, they don't." Heat rose across her cheeks. Was Denise right? Was that what those looks had been about the first morning?

"Oh. My. God. You cannot be that blind."

"Really?" Kat asked. A surge of pleasure zipped through her, making her nipples bead tightly. She could almost picture Kasey and Duncan watching her with Justin. Just the thought made her wet. There was something amazingly powerful about knowing three sexy cowboys all wanted her.

"Come on, Kat, you've been here long enough to have heard all about those three and their exploits."

"Of course I have, but that was different. Justin is happy with things the way they are between us." As close as she'd become with Denise over the past week, it was still weird to talk about her sex life with the other woman. She was Justin's sister for god sakes. It's not as if she could explain to Denise about the way Justin made her feel. No sister wanted to hear that. God, could this get more awkward?

Denise stared down at her feet as she rubbed the back of her neck. "Look, Kat, I really like you and I'd hate to see you get hurt, so umm...crap, I'm just going to say it. My brother doesn't do serious, I know you guys are having fun but...well, I just don't want you to think it's more than it is because chances are with my brother it isn't."

Kat looked around the corral for some way to escape the conversation. "Don't worry, I know the deal with Justin." Even as she said the words a knot formed in Kat's gut. She was such an idiot. Denise was right. If she wasn't careful, she wasn't just going to get hurt, she'd get annihilated by Justin. Despite her best intentions, she was completely falling for him and that was not good. She needed to get her head on straight. This was casual and she needed to remember that.

Denise looked over and flashed a placating smile that said she knew Kat was full of shit. "I'm going to take you up on your offer and grab the first shower," Denise told her, then turned on her boot and walked toward the house.

Deep in thought, Kat slowly wandered into the barn with the saddle. She dumped it on its spot and headed out to grab the rest of the tack. Hauling up the second saddle, she slung it over her shoulder and made her way back to the barn. Kat set the saddle down on top of the stand and fiddled around until it sat properly. She squealed when strong hands gripped her hips tightly.

"Shh, Kat, it's me," Justin's husky voice whispered as he pulled her tighter against him.

She spun around. Lust hit her the moment she looked at him. Quickly followed the litany of Denise's words swirling around in her brain, forcing her to remember this was temporary. "What are you doing back in so early?"

"Shovel broke, I came in to grab another one." He paused and licked his full lower lip, his eyes darkened as he looked down at her. "But now I'm kind of thinking I deserve a quick break."

Kat smirked. Denise might not think she could handle it but she could. Men like Justin didn't come along all that often and she planned to enjoy everything he had to offer. She'd deal with the consequences later. "Oh is that right?"

"Mmm hmm, I've worked really hard today." He caged her in against the saddle she'd just set down.

He bent down and ran his tongue up the column of her neck. Kat's eyes closed and she dropped her head back. She should be embarrassed about letting him kiss her when she was sweaty from working all day but when he moved his hips against her and his hard cock pressed into her belly, she moaned. *Fuck being sweaty.* She wanted to get downright dirty with Justin.

"What did you have in mind for a reward there, cowboy?"

He nipped the soft skin at the base of her ear. "Ever since you arrived here, I've been picturing you like this. Naked. Me fucking you hard against all the tack, or bending you over the saddle rack."

She shivered. Despite the heat of the day, her nipples pebbled against her shirt. "Oh yeah?"

Justin gripped the sides of her snap-closure shirt with both hands. Looking her in the eyes, he pulled, ripping her shirt open all the way down to the bottom. "Damn, Kat, I want to fuck you right now."

Holy cow. She'd never had a man literally rip her clothes off. And Jesus, she liked it. "Then do it," she challenged.

He glanced at the saddle behind her. His nostrils flared and a slow, sexy smile curled up the corners of his lips. "Take off your pants," he ordered.

When he got that dominating tone in his voice, there was no way she could resist. With other guys, that kind of tone turned her off, but with Justin it made everything in her melt. Kat toed off her boots. She flicked open the button on her jeans and shimmied the fabric down her legs.

The moment she stepped out of her pants, Justin gripped her hips, picked her up and set her on the edge of the saddle sideways. Naked from the waist down, she shifted her weight on the seat. The movement made her shirt hang wide open.

Justin's vibrant-blue eyes blazed with arousal as he stared at her, not moving, just looking his fill. Holding out her palm to him, she said, "Come here."

"Hold that thought," he said and jogged off to the little office off the tack room. He returned a few seconds later with the first-aid kit in hand.

Kat raised her eyebrows. What the hell was he doing?

He flipped open the metal lid and triumphantly held up a condom.

"You keep condoms in the first-aid kit?" she laughed.

"It's an emergency kit. It makes sense to be prepared for any emergency." He flashed her a mischievous grin that made her heart pound. *Yeah, way to keep your emotions in check, Kat.* Every time she was with Justin she fell a little deeper into him.

Stalking toward her, he licked his lips. "Now where were we? Oh yeah, I was telling you all about my fantasy of fucking you here in the barn."

The hunger in Justin's eyes made her tremble, moisture pooled in her core. No man had ever made her feel as desirable as Justin did.

Kat held on to the horn with one hand and the back of the saddle with the other and arched her back so her shirt slipped off her shoulders.

"You are so fucking sexy, Kat," Justin growled.

He positioned himself between her legs. The contrast of the warm, soft leather at her ass and the rough fabric of his jeans against her sensitive flesh made her hiss in a breath. He swiveled his hips and she pressed into him, desperate for the contact on her clit. Just the way he looked at her was enough to set her on edge, the slightest touch sent tingles through her body.

Justin licked a path up the column of her neck. "Do you know how many times I've pictured fucking you in here? Pictured fucking you every fucking place on the ranch?" he growled. "Damn it, Kat, I can't stop thinking about you."

The hint of anger in his voice made her lean back to look at him. "Is that a bad thing?" she asked.

"Yeah," he gritted out the words between clenched teeth, as if it pissed him off to admit how much he wanted her.

"Why's that bad?" she asked. Hope blossomed in her gut. Maybe she wasn't the only one feeling this struggle to keep things casual.

He looked at her, his chest rose rapidly as he breathed, his eyes stormed with anger and arousal. "Come on, Kat. What's light about me wanting you every fucking minute of the day?"

She shifted her hips and pressed her body against him. "But I want you just as badly," she whispered and nipped his bottom lip.

He groaned, then his muscular arms banded around her back and pulled her tight against him as his lips crashed down on hers in a kiss she felt all the way to the tips of her toes. The low rumble that rolled from Justin's chest made her pussy clench. God, she loved that sound, so hungry and aroused as if he was fighting for control.

"Fuck me, Justin."

He reached between them and ran his finger down the seam of her pussy. "Jesus," he groaned.

"Just take me hard and fast," she demanded. She needed to feel him inside her, buried deep.

Stepping back, he lowered his jeans, then sheathed himself with the condom. She reached out and pulled him back toward her.

Justin placed his cock at the entrance to her pussy and thrust deep. They both groaned loudly. He paused for a moment, then eased back and thrust forward again. Kat wrapped her legs around his waist and her arms around his neck. The saddle against her ass supported her, angling her hips in such a way that each stroke allowed Justin to hit her G-spot just right.

Kat inhaled deeply, trying to catch her breath. The scent of sex mixed in with the earthy aroma of worn leather. Awareness that they could be caught at any moment added to her arousal.

Justin reached between them and flicked her clit with his finger. Her pussy clenched as the orgasm started to build, her breathing hitched and she moaned. His teeth bit into the soft spot at the base of her neck as he pounded into her. Kat's head dropped back and she closed her eyes as an orgasm ripped through her.

Justin continued to bite her neck as he thrust, dragging out her orgasm as one became another.

"Kat, you're killing me," he groaned as her orgasm pulled him along with her.

He thrust one final time. Her inner muscles continued to clench while her body slowly came down from its high. Boneless, she slumped against him. What was it about Justin that pushed her to do things that she'd never considered doing with anyone else? And each time she did he brought her to new heights. He took her to places she didn't know her body could go.

After several seconds, Justin cleared his throat and stood. "I should, umm, get back to work."

Her mind replayed over the things they'd both admitted in the heat of passion. She'd promised herself she wouldn't get in too deep with him and she was. Trying to keep things light, she smiled. "So, did that live up to the fantasy?"

Justin cleared his throat again. "And then some," he mumbled.

Meeting his stare, she was sure the emotion warring in his eyes matched her own. So much for keeping things simple.

Chapter Seven

After being on the ranch for the past three weeks, Kat had used muscles she didn't even know she had. Leaning her arms on the rails of the porch, she took a sip of her coffee and stared across the expanse of the open range. The sun broke its way over the eastern mountain range, showing off the kind of sunrises she'd only ever heard about back home. She sighed. A girl could get used to this.

The screen door slammed shut, breaking her quiet contemplation. She didn't need to turn to know it was Justin. Every fiber in her body came into awareness the second he was anywhere near her. He set his coffee on the rail beside her.

"Bet you don't see that in New York," he murmured, following her stare to the mountain range.

"There's a lot of things about being here that I don't get in New York," Kat said as her eyes lingered on the corded muscles in Justin's forearms. She loved the way those arms felt wrapped around her, the way they'd rippled beneath her fingers when she touched him.

Justin rested his hand against hers. "Well, if you're game, I was thinking this weekend you could experience a few other things you don't get back in New York."

"Like?"

"I was thinking it might be fun to spend the weekend at the line shack, there's a great fishing hole where we could hang out and do some swimming and fishing."

"Fishing?" she asked and raised her eyebrows at him.

"Among other things."

"What kind of other things?" she purred as she pictured all kinds of naughty possibilities.

Justin pushed off the railing and moved in behind her. His hard muscular chest pressed up against her back. He dipped his head and his breath brushed against her ear. "I was thinking the guys could come with us."

"The guys?" she squeaked.

"Yeah." He sucked her earlobe into his mouth. Kat shivered and tilted her head, not wanting him to stop.

"Kase and Dunc are all over the idea."

Nerves battled with anticipation. "Really? They both want to?"

Justin snorted. "You're sexy as hell. Of course they both want to."

Kat glanced over her shoulder at Justin. "Sexy as hell, huh?"

He gripped her hips and pressed his hard cock against her back. "Feel how hard you get me and I've barely even touched you."

She pressed back and shifted her hips, loving the way he sucked in a breath as she rubbed against him.

He nipped her earlobe. "You like knowing you have that effect on me. Now imagine how that will feel when you have three of us standing there, aching for you."

Justin's fingers slid beneath the waistband of her jeans and slowly eased into her panties. Justin groaned. "Damn, you're wet just thinking about it."

He swirled his finger around her clit and she widened her stance to give him better access.

"Now just imagine how amazing it will feel to be completely filled with aroused male. Duncan in your mouth, Kasey in that hot pussy of yours and me fucking your ass. Would you like that? Being with all three of us at the same time?" He ran his tongue along her neck and nipped the soft spot beneath her ear.

How would it feel to have them all touching her? She longed to see them naked, the contrast between Kasey's bulging muscles and Duncan's whipcord-lean body. Would their cocks match their size? One big and thick, the other long and lean? "Yes," she hissed.

"So you want to?" he asked as he plunged his finger inside her pussy.

"Oh god yes," she groaned.

"All right, I'll talk to them."

Her head snapped up. "What?"

He kissed her lips and nodded. "I'll talk to them about it and get it organized."

"Holy fuck, no. You can't do that." She pulled out of his arms.

"Why? You just said you wanted to." His brow wrinkled in confusion as he stared at her as if he didn't have a clue why she might not be gung-ho.

"Well, Jesus, Justin, there's a big difference between talking dirty about it with you and doing it for real."

"Why? What's the big deal?"

"I don't know. I just—" She took a deep breath. They'd agreed to keep things light between them. Even to her own ears, saying she was scared it would ruin what they had sounded heavy. But damn it, despite her best efforts she was crazy about Justin. She'd meant to keep things purely about sex but somewhere along the line things had changed. She was already dreading going home in three weeks. The last thing she wanted to do was to ruin what little time she had left with him.

Part of her wanted to jump at the chance to live out this fantasy—three sexy cowboys all focused on her. Who wouldn't want that? But what if it ruined everything between her and Justin? As much as she fantasized about the idea of being with all three of them, if things didn't go well and got all awkward, the remainder of her time on the ranch would completely suck.

"What?" Justin asked. "Clearly the idea turns you on so why do you look unsure?"

He turned her around so she was facing him. "What? Talk to me, Kat."

She exhaled audibly. "I like things the way they are between us and I don't want to fuck that up."

Justin's forehead wrinkled as he looked down at her. "Why would it fuck things up?"

"Oh come on, Justin, how could it not?"

He shrugged. "It's sex. It doesn't have to mean any-thing. You have a fantasy, I want to help you live it, nothing wrong with that. You helped me out with that stable fantasy I had, this is no different."

"Yeah right," she scoffed. "Except this time we're inviting your friends to come play."

Justin grinned. "And it will be a lot of fun." When she scowled, he tucked her hair behind her ear and kissed her lightly on the lips. "I know you have concerns and I get that, but trust me. I've done this before and it's not going to fuck anything up for me. Do you think it will for you?"

The fantasy sounded good but a part of her hated the idea that he'd done this before. That he saw her as no different than his buckle bunnies. "I don't know. I don't see why it would, but how can you not look at me differently after I have sex with all three of you at once?"

Justin's cock twitched against her stomach and she glanced down. Justin laughed. "Don't think it's going to be a problem, obviously my body is telling you it likes the idea."

It twitched again and she laughed. "Okay, yeah, it turns you on."

Justin kissed her again. "Let me give this to you."

She glanced up at him and met his stare. "You sure it won't screw things up?"

"It's not going to screw anything up." He cupped her jaw and tilted her head so she was looking at him. "Why don't we all head out tomorrow? The guys will bring their sleeping bags, if you decide you don't want to then they can camp outside instead of in the cabin with us. It's your show, whatever you want goes."

She nervously twirled her hair around her finger. *What if I chicken out?* "And nobody is going to be mad if I decide not to go through with it?"

"Nah, I'm sure the guys will be disappointed because they're already jealous as hell that I get to be with you, but no, they'll understand. We might not be big-city boys but we aren't idiots. We get that this is a big deal to you, but ultimately it's your body so it's your call."

She wrapped her arms around his waist. "Thank you," she murmured. Her mind raced with the possibilities, should she or shouldn't she? How was she supposed to decide this?

Justin tilted her chin up. "But, Kat, the three of us can do things to your body that you never even imagined were possible. With all those extra mouths and hands, we can hit every one of your erogenous zones at one time. You'll be so fucking wet and turned-on, you won't be able to think of anything but how good it feels."

This was a once-in-a-lifetime opportunity—how could she pass it up? She chewed on her lower lip, debating the pros and cons with herself. Finally, she nodded. "Okay."

A huge grin spilt across Justin's face. "Okay." He kissed her. "We're going to give you a weekend you'll never forget."

She needed to create memories that would last her long after she went back to New York. "I'm counting on it."

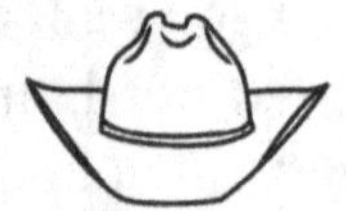

With the wire in his saddlebags, Justin rode back out to meet the guys. He pulled up alongside Kasey as he worked with one of their newer ranch hands, Sam. He dropped off a spool of wire and continued on down the line until he found Duncan working alone digging a new post. Justin hopped off his horse and slid his gloves on his hands.

"About fucking time you got back," Duncan grumbled. He looked Justin over, then said, "What'd you do, take a nap or something?"

Justin grinned.

"You fucker, you went back and had sex, didn't you?" Duncan scowled.

Justin couldn't wipe the grin off his face. "Jealous?"

"Yeah." Dunc shook his head. "The least you can do is dig," he said and handed Justin the shovel.

As they worked side by side fixing the fence, Justin ran over possible ways to bring up the subject of the campout. Justin glanced over at his oldest friend. Man, how many times had they shared a woman? It had always seemed so simple and straightforward, but approaching your buddies about sharing the woman you were dating was somehow different. His dick was certainly all fired up about the idea but he couldn't seem to shut off his brain and its constant commentary that maybe this wasn't such a good idea. That Kat was different.

Justin cleared his throat. The words seemed to be stuck inside.

Dunc glanced over at him. "You all right?"

"Umm...yeah sure..." He cleared his throat again. "Umm...look, the thing is, ugh...well, Kat and I were talking and she's umm..." He rubbed the back of his neck.

"Well, we were thinking of going out to the line shack this weekend and thought maybe you and Kase would want to come along."

"Why do you want us to come with you?" Duncan replied skeptically.

Justin fiddled with the brim of his hat and looked across the open range. "There might be something else on the menu."

Duncan watched him and smirked. "Oh yeah, like what?"

Justin shrugged. "If things go well, then maybe you and Kase could bunk inside with us." He scratched his cheek. Jesus, why was this so hard to say? *Man up, Shaw.* "Kat's got a little fantasy that I thought maybe you two could help me out with."

Duncan turned completely and faced Justin head-on. "Oh really?" Duncan continued to stare at him. "And what about you, Jus, you want that too?"

Justin pushed his hat up on his forehead and rubbed his hand across his face, then pulled the hat back down. "Yeah, what the hell? Why not?"

Duncan continued to stare at him. "You sure? Kat's not like your normal girls."

"I know that," Justin grumbled.

"No, dude, I don't think you do. You're different with her. I've never seen you tangled up about a woman before."

Justin spun the roll of wire in his hands and watched it move. That was exactly why he needed to do this. Things with Kat were intense. Ever since that day in the barn he'd been trying to keep things simple, but spending every night in her bed, seeing her at meals, she was there burrowing a little deeper. He needed to do this to keep things between them all about fun. That's what they'd agreed to. Besides, he really wanted to do this. Watching how hot she got just thinking about being with the three of them completely turned him on. He couldn't wait to see her undone. He hadn't been lying about that. He'd never dated a woman long enough to really dig into her fantasies. Hell, who was he kidding? He never dated a woman long enough to really talk to her. But Kat was different.

Duncan watched him knowingly. "'Cause you seem a little hesitant about the idea, buddy. I mean, I'd be lying if I said I wasn't interested. Kat is hotter than hell but I certainly don't want to do anything to fuck things up between you two."

"Nah, it's cool." *It has to be.*

Finally, Duncan nodded. "All right then, count me in." Duncan stood. "When do we leave?"

Justin laughed. "Not 'til tomorrow, you perv."

Duncan waggled his eyebrows. "Then I guess I'd better get a good night's sleep."

Justin just rolled his eyes at the other man.

That went well, now he just needed to run the idea by Kasey. At the sound of horse hoofs, he looked up. Speak of the devil. Kasey rode up and stopped beside them.

"What's up?" Duncan asked.

"You got any extra water? The dumbass new guy didn't bring enough," Kasey muttered.

"Why didn't Sam come get it himself?" Justin asked.

"Because if I had to stay and listen to him bitch about his girlfriend for another minute he was going to end up being one of the fence posts," Kase complained. "Jesus, you've never seen a guy so wound up about a woman before."

Duncan snorted. Kasey's eyes bobbed between the two men. "What'd I miss?"

"Nothing." Justin scowled.

"Oh come on, Jus, that's not entirely true." Duncan smirked. "Don't you have something you want to ask Kase?"

Justin glared at his best friend, then looked up at Kasey still seated on his horse. "It's no big deal really. I was just talking to Dunc about this weekend." He cleared his throat. "About um...all of us going camping."

"O—kay." Kasey dragged out the word. His brow knit with confusion.

"Our man here wants to do a little group thing with Kat," Duncan jumped in, poking at Justin in that needling way that only old friends could.

Kasey's eyes nearly bugged out at the news. "Seriously?"

Justin shrugged.

"No seriously, you really want us to join you? Are you sure, man? It's Kat."

Justin groaned. Jesus, what was with these two? It really wasn't that big a deal. "Are you in or not?"

Kasey grinned. "Oh hell yeah, I'm in. I just want to make sure you aren't going to get all jealous when she sees my big horse dick and starts to drool," Kasey joked, his eyes lit with amusement as he poked at Justin as well.

Duncan snorted. "You wish you had a horse dick."

Justin groaned. With friends like these two... He shook his head. Needing the conversation to be over, Justin dug out a bottle of water from his saddle bag and tossed it at Kasey. "Get back to work."

Kasey dropped the bottle into his own saddle bag then looked at Justin. "So camping tomorrow?"

"Yeah, but just so you know, if Kat changes her mind you two are sleeping outside," Justin told them.

"No problem, we'll pack our bags in case you or Kat change your mind," Kasey said, making both him and Duncan laugh.

"Get to work. Both of you," he growled. Picking up his shovel, he turned his back on his friends. They were both making way too big a deal of this. He had no intentions of changing his mind. Why would he? Kat and he were just having a good time.

Chapter Eight

As they rode out the next day, Kat couldn't stop thinking about being with all three of them. When did they plan on taking things to the next level? When they stopped for lunch, or would they wait until they got to the cabin? Justin had mentioned stopping and fishing for the afternoon to see what they could catch for dinner, but the little looks the three men kept sending each other made it clear she was the main thing on the menu.

Anticipation bubbled in her stomach. She watched Justin and Duncan riding in front of her, both so powerful and in control. Their muscles rippled as they moved on their horses. She glanced over at Kasey riding contentedly beside her, equally as gorgeous and powerful as the other two men. At the heated look he flashed her, she gulped. *Oh boy.*

When they finally stopped at the edge of a creek bed and dismounted, every muscle in her body was coiled tightly, nerves and sexual excitement battled for supremacy. Was she ready for this?

Kasey took the reins from her and walked the two horses over to where Justin and Duncan had left their mounts.

Kat looked up at the scenery surrounding them. It was gorgeous. The red and copper mountains rose up high, making it seem as if they were the only people on earth. Isolated. She could do anything out here and no one would ever know. Awareness heated her skin as she played over the possibilities in her mind.

Justin walked up to her, took her hand and led her down toward the water. Fallen rocks created a natural dam in the water, leaving a pool behind.

"Is it warm enough to swim?" she asked.

"You bet. Want to jump in?"

"Umm, I didn't bring a suit."

Justin stared at her, his forehead wrinkled with confusion. "And?"

She glanced nervously at Duncan and Kasey. "I don't know."

Justin stepped closer to her and tipped her chin up with his finger. "Did you change your mind?"

She shook her head. "No," she whispered.

Taking her hands in his, he looked down at her. "They're going to see you naked, Kat."

"I know, it's just...I don't... It's broad daylight and I'm dirty and grimy and—" She waved her hand, unsure how to explain what she was feeling.

Duncan and Kasey came up beside them. Kasey looked at Kat and smiled. "Dunc and I were thinking we'd go down a little ways and swim, have some lunch, let you two be alone for a little while."

Kat breathed a sigh of relief. It wasn't that she didn't want to be with them because as she looked over at the two men, lord knew she did. It was just she needed to be with Justin more. She smiled at Duncan and Kasey. "Thanks, guys."

Kasey leaned in and kissed her cheek, his warm lips pressed softly against her skin and she closed her eyes.

When she opened them Kasey winked at her, his golden eyes glimmered with understanding. "No problem, enjoy your swim."

Kat watched as the two men mounted their horses and rode away. Justin's strong arms wrapped around her waist from behind. "You okay?"

"Of course."

"Kat, I told you we weren't going to pressure you at all. This is your call. Whatever you want is fine."

"I know." The guys had ridden around the edge of the rock outcropping until she could no longer see them. She looked at Justin, trying to get a read on him. What was he thinking? Would he be pissed if she backed out? What if not going through with this wrecked things between them anyway? Then she'd still have the next couple of weeks of pure suck to live through.

Justin pulled the ends of her shirt from her jeans. She smacked her hand on top of his. "Hey, what are you doing, mister?"

His nimble fingers reached around her front and undid the buttons of her shirt. "I thought you wanted to go swimming."

"I do."

"Well then, you need to get naked, so I thought I'd help."

If the bulge in his jeans was anything to go by, he didn't seem too disappointed that she'd sent his friends away. "I just bet you did."

He peeled her shirt off her shoulders and dropped it on the ground, then her bra followed suit. She turned around and faced him.

His nostrils flared as he stared at her breasts. Goose bumps shivered across her skin and her nipples tightened from the intensity of his gaze.

"Jesus," he muttered.

Kat toed off one boot, then the other. She stepped back from Justin. "You better catch up, cowboy, otherwise I'll be enjoying myself without you."

"Can I watch?" he asked.

She cocked her hips and flashed him a sassy grin. "Maybe, but you won't be able to see much if you aren't in the water with me."

Justin groaned. "Damn, woman."

He quickly shucked his clothes and stood naked in front of her by the time she managed to shed her jeans. "How the hell did you get undressed so fast?"

"I was highly motivated." Justin took her hand and led her toward the water.

Kat dipped her toe in and winced. Wow, not nearly as warm as she'd anticipated.

She slowly took another step and waited for her feet to get used to the temperature.

"Seriously?" Justin asked.

"What? It's cold," she whined.

Before she had time to even move, strong arms scooped her up and Justin ran into the water with her squealing in protest.

"There, isn't that better?" Justin asked when they were fully immersed in the water. Justin's body was hot against her chest, making the cool water at her back all the more shocking but somehow she didn't mind.

Kat shifted in his arms and wrapped her legs around his waist. She wiggled her hips until she felt his erection press against her bottom. "Mmm, now it is."

She moved again, eliciting a groan from Justin. His hands clamped on to her hips. He shifted his body, dragging his cock along the seam of her pussy.

Justin hoisted her up until her breasts popped out of the water. He bent and ran his tongue across the top of her chest, then slowly swirled his way down until he sucked her nipple into his mouth. Kat arched her back, pressing her nipple deeper inside. The contrast between the cold water and Justin's hot mouth made her pussy clench with need.

He switched to her other nipple. She rubbed her body against his, trying to get the friction she needed to orgasm. Justin stopped and shook his head. "Uh-uh, you aren't getting off that easy. You said you were going to have fun by yourself."

She raised her eyebrow in question as she looked at him. "But you came into the water with me, so I don't need to."

"Need to? No. But I sure as hell would like to see you touch yourself."

Zowie. Her pussy clenched. The idea of masturbating in front of him was a huge turn-on. "Really?"

"Oh yeah," he groaned.

"What did you have in mind?"

"Lady's choice. You know what gets you off, so show me what you like."

She wondered how far away Duncan and Kasey had gone. Would they be able to hear them if she moaned too loud? Her sex throbbed. A dirty little part of her secretly hoped so. With her legs still wrapped around his waist, Kat arched back. She cupped her hand around her breast and pushed it up toward her face. Justin cleared his throat, making Kat grin. If he wanted a show, she'd give him one.

Pushing her breast up as high as she could, she bent her head and stuck out her tongue, flicking it against her nipple.

"Holy fuck," Justin groaned.

Oh yeah, she had him now. His stare was glued to the movement of her tongue. His cock pulsed against her ass and his fingers tightened on her hips.

Justin glanced up and Kat held his gaze while she continued to lick her nipple.

His Adam's apple bobbed as he visibly swallowed. Eyes darkened with lust, his fingers painfully dug into her waist. Just watching her do this was making him lose control. Imagine what he'd be like if he watched her touch herself.

"You like that?" she purred.

"Ye..." He cleared his throat. "Yeah, you could say that."

"What else would you like?" she asked, then playfully sucked her finger into her mouth.

"Jesus, Kat," he muttered. He looked around, then hoisting her up higher in his arms, he walked through the water and set her on the edge of one of the boulders. The hot rock beneath her skin felt amazing. She leaned back against it. Kat brought one knee up and spread her legs. Justin's eyes honed in on her core.

"God, you're gorgeous. Touch yourself," he told her.

Normally when she masturbated, she just went right to her clit but this wasn't about hitting the finish line as quickly as possible. This was about seduction and making Justin squirm. Giving him a taste of his own medicine. She slowly trailed her finger down her body until she hit the little strip of hair. She didn't like to be completely bald. She liked the contrast of the little visible landing strip and the surprise of being completely bare when she spread her legs. Justin watched her with a glazed look in his eyes.

Kat swirled her finger around her clit and sighed. Spreading her lips with one hand, she flicked her clit with the other, loving the way Justin's breathing hitched as he watched. Feeling bold, she pushed her finger inside herself and he groaned. As she fucked herself with her finger, Justin moved closer. His breath burned hot against her leg.

She pulled her finger out of her pussy and placed the digit against his lips. Justin sucked it inside, then growled. Before she had a chance to continue teasing him, he pushed her legs wider, gripped her hips and pulled her against his face. His tongue plunged inside her, sucking and fucking her as if she were his last meal.

After all the teasing she'd just done, the feel of his hot mouth on her core made her squirm with pleasure. She dug her fingers into his thick, chocolate-brown hair and bucked her hips, grinding against his face. "Oh Jus, god, I'm close."

He groaned, the noise vibrated against her clit and she closed her eyes, giving herself over to the pleasure. When he sucked her clit into his mouth, her back arched up off the rock and she screamed. He continued sucking her until she pushed his head away from her. "Stop, I can't take any more."

Justin smirked. "You sure?"

"Yes," she gasped. She closed her eyes and lay boneless on the rock. Thankful she had something to slump against, she was oblivious to the discomfort as she tried to catch her breath.

When she opened her eyes, Justin stared at her with a shit-eating grin on his face. She laughed. "Pleased with yourself?"

"You bet."

He grabbed her hips and pulled her toward him, scraping her ass against the rock. The little bite of pain added to the excitement and the need driving through her. When she hit the water, she squealed. "Holy shit, that's cold."

"Sorry," he murmured as he walked them across the water to the shore. He eased her down on the blanket he'd laid out, then walked over to his saddlebags. A moment later, he was back with a condom in hand.

"There was one in my jeans pocket," she told him.

"We'll use that one later."

Sheathed, he positioned himself between her legs. "Now where was I?"

He pressed against her core and she moaned. "Mmm, that's it, right about there," he groaned as he pushed in.

Kat wrapped her legs around him and dug her heels into his ass to drive him deeper. He thrust and swirled his hips. "Oh Jesus," she groaned. That was the spot. He better not stop.

She threaded her hands through his hair and pulled his face down. His tongue tangled with hers, matching the rhythm of his hips, effectively fucking her face and her pussy at the same time.

She sucked his tongue, eliciting a low, sexy groan that rumbled in his chest. Justin broke the kiss and pounded into her hard, hitting her in all the right spots. Stars burst beneath her lids as another orgasm raced through her body. When she opened her eyes, her nails were digging into Justin's arms and he groaned above her as he came.

Justin collapsed against her briefly, then tried to push up, but she held him tight. "I'm squishing you, Kat."

"No, it's good," she murmured, not wanting to let him go. She sighed. What was wrong with her? She'd always been good at keeping emotions and sex separate. Why was she having such a hard time doing that now?

"Just let me get rid of the condom and then I'll be right back."

She dropped her arms and let him up. God, his ass was spectacular. The muscles flexed and rippled as he walked to his saddlebags again and pulled out a plastic bag for garbage and disposed of the condom. She continued to stare at his body when he walked back toward her with a cooler bag in his hand.

"Obviously, I didn't do a good enough job, since you still look like you want a piece of me," Justin teased.

"I always want a piece of you." Unfortunately, that was the problem. How was she supposed to go back to New York in a couple of weeks and not think about him?

"Give me a minute and you can." He dropped down beside her and sat crossed-legged as he dug into the cooler bag. He handed her a turkey sandwich and a Coke.

Kat sat up and took a bite of her sandwich. It should have felt weird sitting naked outside eating but it didn't. Somehow, Justin made it seem the most natural thing in the world.

"So, do you ever miss traveling and doing the full-time rodeo tour thing?"

"Nah, I only really did it for money. I mean it was fun, and I got to travel and see things, but at the end of the day it was a just a means to an end."

"What do you mean?"

He shrugged. "This is home and I needed enough money to make it into what I wanted."

"How did you want it?"

He absently pulled a thread on the blanket. "Growing up, Dee and I had plans for this place. We were sure we could make it into this amazing thing." He smiled to himself. "Dee has a real gift with horses. Well, you know what she can do. I've never seen anyone like her. She'd always dreamed of being a trainer." He laughed but the sound was sad and empty, not like his normal laugh. "Our dad was against the idea. So I let her use the little chunk of land I'd been given for my twenty-first birthday."

"Your sister didn't get any land on her twenty-first?"

"God no. The ol' man would never have done that." He absently drew a pattern on the blanket with his finger as he talked. "Anyways, she had the land but even with that my dad wouldn't give her any money to fund her little hobby as he called it..." He paused.

His dad sounded like such a jerk. Good thing she'd never met him or she'd have had a few things to say to the chauvinistic asshole. "So?"

Justin looked up, blushed and looked down again. Kat's heart clenched when she saw the color on his cheeks. God, how could she not completely fall for a guy who loved his sister as much as Justin did?

"So, she needed capital to make the business a success. I joined the circuit to get that for her, for us, for our family."

"And she started her business."

He raised his head. "Yeah. Man, you should have seen her. She had people lining up right off the bat. My old man was pissed." He laughed.

"Pissed, why?"

"Because she was earning her own money, and she was busy doing her own thing." He shook his head. "A man shouldn't have to hire strangers to come into his house to cook and clean when he has a daughter who can do the work." Justin made his voice gritty in what she had to assume was an imitation of his dad.

"Oh he did not say that."

"Sure did. A woman's place is in the kitchen, didn't you know?" His eyes twinkled with amusement.

"Fuck that," she muttered.

Justin laughed. "No wonder you and Dee get along so well. Anyway, when my dad died, I quit the circuit, came home and took over the ranching side of things, so Dee could focus on her training. Dunc and Kasey came with me to work, since they were tired of traveling around all the time."

"Have you made changes to the ranch since you took over?"

"Yeah, like I said, Dee and I dreamed big, that's why I still do some bull riding and stuff to earn some extra cash."

"I thought you just did that for fun."

"That too, but there're some damn good purses up for grabs. The money goes a long way. That's kind of why the guys and I still do the rodeo thing when the mood strikes."

"Does the mood strike often?"

"Not as often as it used to," he replied.

"How's the purse at the one at Madison Square Garden?"

"It's decent, why?"

"Just wondering if you ever make it to New York." If he did, then maybe things didn't have to completely end for good when she had to leave.

"You never know." He shifted and moved closer to her, his lips an inch away from hers.

"Hold that thought," she said and stood. Kat grabbed her jeans and slid them on.

"What are you doing?" Justin sat up and stared at her, confusion etched across the lines of his face.

Heat rose up her cheeks. God, this was embarrassing. "I just have to take care of business."

"Okay. But why are you getting dressed?"

"Well, I'm not just going to go wandering around naked."

"Where are you wandering to?"

"I don't know. Someplace where you can't see me."

Justin rolled his eyes. "I will never understand the way a woman's mind works. I'm glad I'm a guy."

"Me too," Kat replied.

Justin laughed. "Get going and hurry back."

Chapter Nine

Kat readjusted her clothes. Sometimes it sucked being a woman. A guy could just whip it out wherever he was while she'd had to tromp halfway across the state to ensure she had some privacy to do her business.

She stepped out from behind the rock cropping and grimaced. Crap, it all looked exactly the same. What the hell had she been thinking, wandering so far away? There wasn't an inch of her body the man hadn't seen. Would it really have been such a big deal if he'd seen her squatting in the bush? *Yeah, it would.*

She wandered past a few rocks looking for something familiar and faintly heard voices off in the distance. Following the sound, she rounded a boulder and stopped dead in her tracks.

Sweet mother of god, she knew she should look away but she was unable to pull her eyes off the sight in front of her.

Kasey and Duncan, naked and aroused, stood a hairs-breadth away from each other. Their hair dripping from their own dip in the water, their clothes lay in a pile on the ground beside them. As she watched, Duncan gripped Kasey's hips and pulled him against his body and into a searing, hungry kiss. Kasey shifted his stance and Duncan moved his hips in a circular motion so their cocks rubbed together. When they broke apart, she could see the rapid rise and fall of their chests.

They were spectacular. There was a hungry desperation to their touch but as they stood looking at each other, she could see the connection and caring between the two men from her spot several yards away. An intensity hummed through the air that spoke of something so much deeper than a mindless fuck. They had a connection she'd never experienced with anyone, except maybe Justin.

As she watched, Duncan ran his tongue along Kasey's chest. Kasey's hands wove into Dunc's sun-streaked hair. The muscles in Kase's arms flexed as if he was guiding Duncan's movements lower. She heard the low, masculine chuckle that rumbled and could only guess that the sound came from Duncan as he spun Kasey around and both men dropped to their knees on the pile of clothing. Duncan reached around and gripped Kasey's cock in his hand and muttered something Kat couldn't quite hear. Kasey's head dropped back against his shoulder.

Kat looked around. What the hell was wrong with her that she couldn't take her eyes off them? She knew she should leave and not watch but she couldn't help herself. The sight of the two men wrapped around each other, tongues battling for supremacy, was the hottest thing she'd ever seen. She leaned against the side of the rock. Needing to ease the ache between her legs, she slid her hand down the front of her jeans. Her panties were soaking wet just from watching them. Eyes wide open, glued to the scene in front of her, she dipped her finger inside herself and bit back a groan. A warm hand encased her hip and she jumped, the hand covering her mouth the only thing that kept her scream from being heard.

"Shh, it's just me," Justin whispered against her ear. The feel of his hot breath against her skin sent a shiver racing through her, coating her finger with arousal.

Justin glanced at the couple in front of them, then back at Kat and wrinkled his nose. "That works for you?"

She watched Kasey as he ran his tongue along the shaft of Duncan's cock, Dunc's hands fisted in Kasey's hair and his head tipped back, exposing the long line of his throat.

Afraid that if she spoke, Kasey and Duncan would hear her, she nodded in response. Heat blazed across her face. She could only imagine what Justin must be thinking about her.

Justin grabbed her wrist and pulled her hand from her pants and sucked the digit inside. "Damn, Kat, you're fuckin' soaked." His chest rumbled quiet and low, a warning as he swooped in, his mouth hot, demanding on her lips as he pressed her back against the rock.

He gripped the waist of her jeans and shoved them down only to have them get hung up on her boots. God, she wanted him inside her. Right now. Too impatient to wait for him, she spun out of his arms and placed her hands on the edge of the boulder and pressed her ass out against his cock, leaving no question as to what she wanted.

She opened her eyes and could just see Kasey and Duncan from their hidden location. Kasey on his hands and knees with Duncan poised behind him, working him hard. She gasped as another wave of arousal shot through her.

"Fuck me, Jus," she whispered hoarsely and wiggled her hips. He stuck his finger in her back pocket and pulled out the condom she'd mentioned earlier. She heard the sound of a wrapper ripping, then finally, he placed his cock against her pussy. Her head dropped forward and she pressed against him, needing him buried inside her.

"Impatient, aren't you?" The low, whispered growl vibrated against her spine. "Let's just see if you like to be ridden as hard as you're asking for."

He wrapped his hand around her braid and pulled her head back, forcing her ass to push farther away from the rock. God, she loved having her hair pulled, the way that Justin controlled her movements using her hair like reins. He thrust into her in one long, hard, deep thrust and she bit back her moan. His thick cock filled her completely. She rested an elbow on the rock to hold herself up and reached between her legs to flick her finger against her clit.

Kat turned her head and watched Duncan and Kasey as Justin pounded into her. She would never have thought watching someone having sex would turn her on so damn much. Hell, she didn't even like to watch porn, but something about the primal, raw need between the two men was hotter than anything she'd ever seen. What would it feel like to be able to join in? To have all that hot male arousal focused on her? *Amazing.*

Justin's teeth bit into her neck. He left his head buried there, not watching the display in front of them but focused completely on her. His fingers bit into her hips as he thrust. Kat bit her lower lip to keep herself quiet as the intensity of her orgasm tore through her. The last thing she wanted was Kasey and Duncan hearing her. Biting back her moans of pleasure as her orgasm started to build, she dropped her head against the rocks, her eyes glazed, no longer able to focus on watching the other two men as she concentrated on what Justin was doing to her body. The orgasm that tore through her seemed to go on and on. If it wasn't for the rock beneath her elbow, she would have collapsed under its intensity. Justin thrust into her several more times, then she felt his body shudder behind her as he came.

After adjusting himself back into his jeans, Justin watched Kat fix her own clothing. Half of her hair stuck out of her braid from his firm grasp. He winced, wondering if maybe he'd been a little rougher with her than he should have been. But finding her masturbating had instantly made him hard. Watching Kasey and Duncan didn't do anything for him, but when he'd touched her pussy and found it dripping wet... That had more than worked for him.

He glanced over at his two friends. He'd known for some time now that Kasey and Duncan liked to hook up occasionally. He honestly hadn't expected them to take off and fuck, but now that he thought about it, it kind of made sense. Hell, they'd left to give him some privacy with Kat, it only made sense that they'd take advantage of the opportunity.

Not wanting to be caught watching them, Justin grabbed Kat's hand and pulled her back toward their earlier picnic. Once they were away from earshot, he turned to her.

"So, turns out there's a lot more to you than meets the eye."

Her cheeks burned red and she looked briefly at him, then her eyes focused on something toward the mountain. "Yeah, about that...umm...I'm not really even sure what to say. I'm kind of embarrassed that you caught me...well, masturbating while I watched them after I made such a big deal about them seeing me skinny-dip." She laughed nervously.

He stepped toward her and cupped the back of her neck. "Don't be. You've got nothing to be ashamed of. If it works for you, it works for you. No shame in that." He pressed his lips against hers and whispered, "Besides, it was hotter than shit seeing you like that, so I'm sure not complaining."

She peeked up at him. "Really?"

Even just thinking about it now turned him on. What he'd really like was to see her spread out on his bed naked, with her hand between her legs touching herself until she came, his cock in her mouth and his friends each sampling her body as well. Just the idea made him hot and if she gave him a couple of minutes, he'd show her exactly how much it turned him on. "Yeah."

Kat held his gaze, her eyes darkened as she looked at him. "I'm glad you found me, though. It was so much better with the real thing rather than the fantasy."

He placed his hand on her hip and pulled her against him. "Oh yeah, so what exactly were you fantasizing about?"

She blushed again. Justin raised an eyebrow at her. Just what was that look about, he wondered.

"Were you picturing yourself in one of their places?" he asked.

"No...not really." She licked her bottom lip. "Honestly, what ended up happening was pretty much the fantasy. I've never really watched someone have sex before and it kind of surprised me how hot it was." Her tongue dipped out again. "Having you touching me just made it that much better."

He nipped her earlobe and sucked it inside his mouth, enjoying the way she sagged against him and shivered. She was always so damn responsive. "So you didn't wish that you were sandwiched between them and all that attention was focused on you?" he whispered.

Kat dropped her head against his chest. "N-no," she stammered.

"No?"

She shook her head weakly.

"But the idea turns you on?" he asked.

She didn't meet his eye but she nodded.

He shifted so her legs were on either side of his thigh as he pulled her tighter against him and cupped her ass. "And what if I was there, too? Would you like that? All three of us focused completely on you. Playing with your nipples, your pussy, your ass."

She groaned loudly and rubbed her pussy against his thigh, riding his leg. He eased his hand down the back of her jeans and cupped her ass.

"Come on, you know you want to," he said.

She looked around. "What would people think?"

He laughed. "Umm...look around, Kat. Not a lot of people out here to see." He waved his arm out toward the wide open spaces surrounding them. Mountains on one side, open fields on the other. "How the hell would anyone know what we did out here? Do you think anyone actually knows that Dunc and Kase fuck each other?"

She shrugged. "Don't they?"

"Fuck no. Cowboy code isn't really all that forgiving of guy on guy. It's not done, and if it is, it's sure as shit not talked about."

"But why?"

"I don't know." He shrugged. "It just isn't."

She glanced toward the mountains they had just come from. "If they're a couple, what makes you think they'd even be interested in being with us?"

Justin snorted. "It's not really an 'us' being offered here, darlin', it's just you. I'm cool with Dunc and Kase swinging both ways, but I don't." He ran his eyes down her body, taking in the curve of her waist and her ample breasts. "Believe me, they're interested—they're just waiting for me to give them a chance."

She wiped her palms against her jeans. "So they're bi or something?"

"Or something." He ran his hand through his hair. Shit, he didn't really want to talk about his friends having sex with each other. "You saw them leaving with that girl at the dance. They've done the whole threesome thing before, you know that." He thought back to the day they'd all met Kat and the way his friends had been eyeing her up. When he'd mentioned the possibility, they'd practically stampeded him to pack their bags. Oh hell yeah, they'd be all over the chance to be with her.

He ignored the little niggle of doubt that asked him if he knew what he was doing and pushed on. "Look, we're miles from anyone else. We're staying up here in the line shack tonight anyway, so why don't we just enjoy what the night can bring. You know what happens on the range stays on the range." He waggled his eyebrows at her.

Kat's brow furrowed as she looked at him. "So how would this work? Would I fuck you all? Or would they fuck each other and you'd fuck me?"

He groaned. God, typical woman, talking things to death. Her nipples pressed tightly against her top as her chest rose rapidly. Clearly, the idea turned her on. Why not just go with it?

"I don't know. I can't imagine them fucking each other since they don't do that with other people watching." He laughed. "Well, normally."

Her eyes darkened as she looked at him. "Do you think they would if we asked?"

He rubbed his hand over his face and groaned. "Jesus, I don't know. Do you really need them to?" Christ, it was one thing to know his friends did that, or even to see it out of the corner of his eye from a distance. It was a whole other thing to have it happening while you were all in bed together.

"Never mind," Kat said.

Stepping toward her, he wrapped his arm around her waist. "Why don't we play it by ear. I'll let them know you're up for them joining us tonight and we'll see how things go." He kissed her lips and she trembled against him. Damn, she was so hot and ready for anything. He'd never met a woman he was so sexually compatible with. Too bad their relationship had such a short shelf life. "What do you say?"

"You sure you'd be cool with them joining us?" she asked.

He frowned at her. "Why wouldn't I be?"

Kat shrugged. "I don't know, in theory it always sounds good, but I'd imagine it could get kind of messy."

"Relax, Kat, we've all done this before."

"Yeah, but wasn't that usually with someone a little more casual? I mean, not that we're serious or anything because I know this is just temporary but..."

He kissed her. "You think too much. There's nothing to worry about."

"You sure? Because I don't need to do this. It's a fantasy but certainly not one I ever planned on living out." She twirled her hair in that cute little nervous way of hers as she watched him.

"Darlin', prepare for the fantasy of your life." Cupping the back of her neck, he pulled her against him and kissed her.

The sound of a throat clearing broke them apart. Justin glanced over at the amused smirks of his two best friends. Anyone looking at them would never suspect that just minutes ago they'd been devouring each other.

"So you two just about ready to get back to work? We've got dinner to catch," Duncan said.

Kat blushed when she looked at the other two men. Justin wrapped his arm around her shoulder. "What do you mean? We've been working while you two were slacking off. Right, Kat?" Justin asked, grinning when the pink on her cheeks deepened to a bright red.

Duncan flashed Kasey a look, then turned his attention back at them. "So you've caught dinner then?"

"Umm, no," she mumbled.

Kasey burst out laughing. "Didn't think so."

Justin squeezed Kat's shoulders. "Come on, woman, the faster we get finished, the faster we can finish this discussion."

Kat flicked a glance at the other two men and blushed again.

Justin winked at Kat. *Oh yeah, this was going to be fun.*

Chapter Ten

At the cabin later that evening, Justin walked up behind Kat and wrapped his arm around her waist. He leaned in close and whispered, "They're in."

She whipped around and stared at him. Her eyes widened as anxiety and arousal warred with each other in the hazel depths.

"You still want to?" he asked.

Kat blew out a deep breath, then nodded. "You sure this is a good idea?"

"I'm sure." He placed a quick kiss against her lips. "I told you we've all done this before so there're no surprises for me. The ball's completely in your court."

Her gaze stayed glued to him for several seconds, then finally she nodded. "Let's do it."

A slow grin split across his face. He couldn't wait to see her spread out before them, with each of his friends feasting on her sexy body as she sucked his cock. He glanced over at Kasey and nodded. Kase smiled and stood. He walked toward them. Kat tensed beside him. "Relax, sugar," Justin whispered in her ear.

Kasey stopped in front of them and tipped Kat's chin up with his finger. "You sure you want this, Kat? You look like a little baby calf going into the chute."

The staccato beat of her heart pulsed visibly at the base of her neck. "I want to. I've just never done anything like this before, I'm not really sure what to expect."

Duncan came in from the makeshift shower outside, his towel wrapped around his waist, water dripped down the ridges of his muscular abdomen and both Kasey's and Kat's eyes darkened with arousal.

Dunc stopped and stood looking at the group. "What?"

"Good shower?" Kasey asked.

"Relaxed me a little, yeah," Duncan replied and winked.

"So judging by the way you are all looking at me, can I assume Kase and I are going to be allowed to bunk in here tonight?"

All three men turned and looked at Kat. Finally, she nodded.

"This is your fantasy, Kat, what do you want to have happen?" Justin asked her.

She looked at Duncan and Kasey, then at Justin and she blushed.

"What, honey?"

"Will you two kiss?" she asked, looking at Duncan and Kasey.

"What?" Kasey asked. His eyes flickered anxiously to Duncan, then back at Justin and Kat.

Justin laughed. "Dude, she knows about you two."

"What do you mean she knows?"

"We saw you this afternoon," Kat replied.

"Fuck," Kasey groaned.

Duncan shrugged his shoulders, as if being caught didn't matter to him at all.

"What exactly did you see?" Kasey asked.

Justin coughed, embarrassed to have to tell his two best friends he'd seen them fucking.

"Jus," Kasey demanded.

Heat swept across Justin's cheeks. He cleared his throat. "We um...saw you ummm..." he stammered.

"We saw you having sex," Kat said, saving Justin from spelling it out.

"You did?" Kase asked. Justin could feel his two best friends staring at him, so he raised his head and nodded.

"And we're cool?" Kasey's eyes were wide with nerves as he looked at him. Justin's stomach clenched. Did they honestly think he was that big of an asshole that he'd really care? "Why wouldn't we be? It's not like I just found out about you two. Hell, I've walked in on you two fucking before. It wasn't exactly a shock this time."

Kasey stared at him for a few seconds, his brow wrinkled with concern as he rubbed the back of his neck. Then he nodded.

Duncan stepped closer to Kat. "I thought this was about you, Kat, so why do you want to see Kase and I kiss?"

Justin could practically feel the heat coming off her as she blushed. "It was hot," she murmured.

"What was hot?" Duncan asked.

"Watching you two together—" She shrugged. "It worked for me."

Duncan grinned, then met Justin's eyes over her head. "I know it doesn't work for you, so are you cool with it, or is it going to turn your dick into a limp noodle?"

Trust Duncan to get to heart of things. Justin laughed. "I think I'll manage."

Kat glanced at him over her shoulder. "It didn't seem to be a problem earlier."

"That had more to do with you fingering yourself than them fucking, darlin'," he said and nipped her shoulder.

Duncan and Kasey shared a look. Heat flared between them, it was almost tangible and Kat shivered in his arms. "You sure you're okay with having a front-row seat though?" Duncan asked Justin.

"As long as you boys keep your hands off me, we're all good."

Kasey snorted. "Yeah, don't flatter yourself, dude. I've got zero desire to touch you." Kasey placed his hand under Kat's chin and looked down at her. "But you," he said and tipped her face toward him. "You, I definitely want to touch."

Kasey wrapped his hands around the back of Kat's neck and pulled her to him. He kissed Kat softly and with a lot more gentle care than Justin ever did. Shit, maybe he was too rough with her. Not that she ever complained. She matched him stroke for stroke. But as he watched her kiss Kasey, he felt a little niggle of insecurity that maybe she needed that gentle tenderness too. Shit, he needed a drink. There was a reason they'd never done this completely sober before. It was a bit weird.

When the kiss broke, Kat looked over at Justin and smiled shyly.

"What do you say we have a couple of drinks and relax a little?" he suggested.

Kat's shy smile blossomed into a full-out grin. "A drink would be good."

He cracked the top off a beer and handed it to her. Kat brought the bottle to her mouth and damn near drained the whole thing in one long gulp. A couple more drinks and any nerves or unease any of them were feeling would completely disappear.

She set her empty bottle on the counter and turned around. The intensity of all three men staring at her made Kat shiver with desire. Her nipples pebbled against the fabric of her bra. Nerves battled with arousal and she felt like an erotic mess.

She didn't know if she should bury her head in the sand or rip off all her clothes and jump on the near-est available cock. Justin was right, this was her fantasy and no one would ever find out if she didn't tell them. Lord knows she had fantasized about this enough times, granted normally she pictured two guys not three. The possibilities made her mouth go dry.

All three men stared at her. Three of the sexiest men she had ever laid eyes on all wanted her. There was no way she was going to pass that up. With her mind made up, she reached for the bottom of her shirt, peeled it over her head and dropped it on the floor.

When she glanced at the men, Justin grinned at her and quickly followed suit, tossing his shirt aside as well. Movement flickered against Duncan's towel as his dick flared to life. Feeling even bolder, Kat peeled her jeans down her thighs and kicked them out of the way. She stood before the three men clad only in her bra and panties.

She reached out her hand for Justin, needing the reassurance of his touch. He immediately came to her and wrapped his arms around her waist from behind, engulfing her in his warm, comforting embrace, solidifying them as a unit.

Crooking her finger, she beckoned the other two men over. Kasey and Duncan stopped in front of her. She trailed the tips of her fingers down the front of Kasey's chest. He inhaled audibly and his stomach muscles clenched at the contact. She grinned and did the same thing to Duncan. His dick twitched beneath the towel, flicking the fabric as if to demand attention as well. Justin lifted her hair off her shoulder and placed a kiss against her neck.

With Justin at her back and Kasey and Duncan pressing up against her front, she was sandwiched between three aroused males. God, how did she even decide where to start? Duncan titled her chin toward him and took the decision out of her hands.

His kiss was firmer than Kasey's had been, more demanding. She wondered if he would kiss Kasey the same way. Lord, she wanted to see them together. Cupping the back of Kasey's head, she pulled him toward her. When her kiss broke with Duncan Kasey immediately took his place. The contrast between firm and demanding and soft and sensual was more than she could take. She didn't know which way was up.

She turned her head to Justin, needing to feel the grounding effect of his kiss. The moment his lips touched hers, his tongue pressed inside, claiming her, and she melted back against him.

Breathing hard, they parted. She looked at Duncan and Kasey who were hungrily watching her. She placed her hand on the back of each of their heads, guiding their mouths together. Their tongues tangled. The kiss was so much rougher and more aggressive than what either of them had done to her. She couldn't take her eyes off them.

Justin bent and ran his tongue along the length of her back, licking his way up from the base of her spine all the way up to her neck. She widened her legs and he chuckled behind her.

He stood and took her hand and led her to the makeshift bed on the floor, then turned to his friends and whistled to get their attention. The two men broke apart, both breathing rapidly.

"Wow, that was hot," Kat murmured.

Duncan grinned and slowly stalked toward her on the floor. "You liked that, did you?"

"Ohmigod yeah." Her head bounced like a bobble-head as she nodded in agreement.

Kat got up on her knees and looked at the couple. "Ditch the pants and come here," she demanded.

The two men stood in front of her, gloriously aroused, their hard cocks stood proudly out from their bodies. She wrapped her right hand around Kasey's shaft. It was so thick her finger couldn't even touch her thumb when she closed her palm around him. Her mouth watered as she looked at it. Wrapping her left hand around Duncan's cock, she sighed. The long, smooth shaft throbbed against her palm. Giving two guys head at the same time seemed so wicked and dirty.

She felt Justin kneel on the mattress behind her. He ran a hand down the length of her back, then trailed his finger through the seam of her ass. His tongue followed the path of his hand. Light, teasing nips bit into her cheeks and she groaned.

The cocks in front of her eyes bobbed, demanding attention. Kat ran her tongue along the column of Duncan's penis, then switched to Kasey's. Strong hands wrapped into her hair, another pair gripped her shoulders while Justin's finger swirled around her clit. Holy hell. She inhaled deeply, the scent of hot, aroused man filled her senses.

She licked the tip of the thick cock in her hand and nibbled the head with her lips. When Justin's tongue ran up the seam of her ass, she moaned and fully swallowed Duncan's cock.

"Jesus, Kat," Dunc groaned.

She trailed her tongue up along the shaft. Duncan thrust forward, driving his cock to the back of her throat. He eased out, then forward again. Beside him, Kasey growled, drawing her attention back to him. She released Duncan's cock with a pop and smiled at Kasey. "Sorry, were we neglecting you?"

"Little bit." As he looked down at her and smiled, his hazel eyes looked almost a chocolate brown with arousal.

The head of his cock glistened with pre-cum and she slowly licked the tip, then swirled her tongue around the head. Keeping her eyes on the two men in front of her, she moaned when Duncan pulled Kasey's head toward him and ground their lips together.

She dimly registered the sound of a wrapper being opened behind her, then strong hands gripped her hips and she closed her eyes as Justin placed the head of his cock against her pussy. She pressed back into him.

Kasey slid out of her mouth, and she hissed, "Yes," as Justin thrust into her, seating himself fully. He felt amazing. Justin swiveled his hips and thrust again, hitting her G-spot.

Kat kept her eyes closed, enjoying the sensation of the men surrounding her. A cock hit her lips, nudging for entrance. She sucked it inside, allowing Justin to set the rhythm. When he pulled from her, she slid back, letting his forward thrust ram the cock into her mouth.

"Fuck," Kasey gritted. His hand wrapped around hers, clamping their palms together around Duncan's shaft, working in tandem to keep up a steady rhythm on him as well. Kat opened her eyes. The two men continued to kiss as Kasey fucked her mouth and Duncan fucked their hands.

Justin's rough, calloused hand slid around her stomach and down until he reached her clit. He pressed against the tight button and her pussy clenched. God, that felt amazing, but then every time Justin touched her was amazing.

Fingers pressed against her head as the men broke their kiss. "You need to stop, I'm close," Kasey told her.

Kat paused, then sucked him deeper into her mouth. He inhaled audibly as if the move took his breath. He dug his fingers into her scalp and thrust toward her. He came with a loud, long groan. Kat swallowed, savoring every drop of his arousal.

When she sat up, Duncan was working his shaft, since Kat and Kasey had stopped. Kat grimaced. "Sorry," she said, feeling guilty they'd left him to his own devices.

"No worries, darlin'. You can make it up to me later," Duncan grunted. He angled his body away from her and came on the floor beside her. Jesus, that was hot.

With both men taken care of Kat was able to completely focus on her own orgasm.

"Now you're all mine," Justin growled. He thrust into her deep, bottoming out. He pinched her clit between his fingers and stars burst behind her eyelids. Kat dropped her head forward, gasping for breath as Justin continued to use her hard. He didn't let up. His finger swirled around her clit. Leaning down, he bit the sensitive spot on her neck and the end of the first orgasm drove forward into her second.

Justin groaned and thrust one more time, then shuddered above her as his own orgasm took him. She collapsed onto the floor. Holy shit, that was better than anything she could have imagined. Her jaw ached from the awkward angle she'd had to hold her head to suck Kasey's thick cock but it was a good ache. By the end of the weekend, she hoped to be a lot more sore, she thought and smiled to herself.

Justin placed a kiss against the small of her back, then hopped up to dispose of his condom. A second later, he was back beside her.

Kasey's stomach rumbled. He slapped his palm against his abs and Kat burst out laughing. Something so simple as a rumbly tummy somehow made the moment seem so completely normal.

Kat pushed herself up. "All right, let's get you guys fed because I have plans for the rest of the night." This was her one chance to live out the fantasy. She planned to make the most of it.

Chapter Eleven

Duncan stood and walked over to his saddle bags and rooted around. Naked, he turned and triumphantly held up a big bottle of tequila. "Anybody up for some shots?"

Kat grinned. "Count me in."

Dunc plopped the bottle down on the little counter and pulled some cups out of his bag. The man really came prepared.

She pushed herself up and reached for Justin's discarded shirt. Kasey's hand slapped down on hers. "Uh-uh, honey, no need to get dressed."

Kat chewed her lower lip and eyed the three perfect male specimens in front of her. They seriously expected her to wander around, drinking and eating, naked. She glanced over at Justin who shrugged.

"I'm definitely going to need a shot," she groaned.

No sooner had she said the words than Duncan handed her a cup with a shot of tequila. She downed it in one gulp, feeling the burn as it made its way down her throat to her gut. "Holy crap," she muttered when she could finally speak.

Justin laughed. "Ah, Dunc must have brought the good stuff."

Kat eyed her empty glass. They had different definitions of good tequila.

Justin placed a kiss on her lips, then pushed himself off the floor. "All right, who's cooking?" he asked.

The three men pulled out the big guns to decide. After a rousing battle of rock, paper, scissors, Kasey emerged as the loser. With the lighter in hand, he fired up the portable BBQ on the counter.

With the grill lit, he turned to look at the others. "Are you guys seriously going to let me do everything?"

Justin and Duncan shrugged. "Well, you did lose," Justin replied.

Kat rolled her eyes. Men. She stood and walked toward Kasey. His eyes tracked her body as she moved, naked, across the room. "I'll help you," she said when she stopped in front of him

Kasey grinned. He wrapped an arm around her waist and pulled her against his hard, muscular body. "Thank you, darlin'," he murmured, then pressed his lips against hers.

When they pulled apart, Duncan and Justin were no longer sitting on the floor but had joined them in the kitchen. Kat took one look at the lust on their faces and held up her hand. "Oh no you don't. You guys are feeding me before we do anything else."

Justin trailed his hand down her spine, leaving goose bumps pooling along her back. "You sure? Kase could cook and we could work up more of an appetite while we wait."

God that sounded good. She glanced over at Duncan who grinned as if that was the best idea he'd ever heard, then at Kasey who, bless him, was pouting as if he'd had his favorite toy broken. Kat laughed. She didn't have the heart to do that to Kase.

She patted Kasey on the cheek. "Don't worry, big guy, we won't make you do all the work."

Kasey kissed her again. "Appreciate it," he told her.

Justin shook his head. "Man, you and that pathetic doe-eyed look. You fucked me again." Justin punched Kasey on the arm and laughed.

Kasey rubbed his shoulder. "It's not my fault Kat has a soft heart."

Kat laughed at the byplay between the men. Their ease with each other made any lingering discomfort she felt about the situation disappear.

After dinner, Kat picked up what was left of the bottle of tequila and looked at it. Holy crap, they'd put quite a dent in it over dinner. She took a step, swayed and giggled. Okay, apparently she'd done her part to drain it.

With the bottle in hand, she carried it and the cups back over to the makeshift bed. "All right, let's play a little drinking game."

She looked over her shoulder at the three men who were all staring at her ass as she walked. She crawled on hands and knees over to claim her spot on the bed. Various muttered oaths and groans sounded as she crawled. Men were so easy.

"You boys coming?"

"Almost," Duncan muttered.

Kat grinned. "Well then, why don't we get started on this drinking game, and we'll see if we can't take care of that for you."

The three men joined her on the bed. As they sat, all three of their cocks stood at attention. Kat licked her lips. *Yummy.*

"What kind of game did you have in mind?" Justin asked.

"Well, I was thinking a little game of spin the bottle."

Justin looked around the circle and raised one eyebrow at her. Kat giggled again. "No, don't worry, I wasn't expecting that. It's a drinking game. So if you spin and don't want to kiss the person you land on then you drink."

Duncan cocked his head and looked at her. "But, honey, then you'll never drink."

"I know." She licked her lips. "You guys will just have to make it up to me."

Kasey reached over and grabbed the empty beer bottle off the floor. "All right, I'm in. Who's first?"

"You've got the bottle, so why don't you go?" she replied.

These guys were great, so much fun. She was really going to miss them when she had to leave. They weren't at all like the guys she knew back home who were so uptight. Never taking a moment to just have fun in case they missed the next big deal, their cell phones attached like a limb no matter what they were doing. Out here, it was different. She was surprised by how much she enjoyed the laid-back lifestyle. They worked hard. Hell, harder than she'd ever imagined, but at the end of the day when they were there with you, they were really there with you. Not wishing they were someplace else, earning another dollar.

Kasey set the bottle on the bed and spun. The bottle pointed at Dunc. The two men looked at each other then Kasey slid over and gripped the back of Duncan's neck firmly, holding his head in place. Heat flared in Duncan's eyes at the possessive look on Kasey's face. Kat squirmed as she watched the subtle power struggle between the two men. Wasn't Duncan the more dominant one? Did it work that way? She'd always thought one guy was always the top and one always the bottom, but as she looked at them she wondered if that was always the case. It would sure be hot to find out.

After an all-too-brief kiss, in Kat's mind, Duncan took the bottle from his partner and spun it. It didn't move all that easily and got jumbled up in the blanket, making it point at Justin.

"Oh hell no," Justin muttered.

"You got that right," Duncan replied with a laugh. He filled his cup with tequila and shot it back, then handed the bottle to Justin.

Justin spun. It landed on her. A smile split across his face. "I think I'm going to like this game," he murmured as he cupped the back of her head and drew her toward him.

"Me too," she whispered just before his lips touched hers. Unlike the high school spin the bottle game, Justin didn't just give her a light kiss and pull away. He held her there, deepening the kiss until he pulled her under. When they broke apart, they were both panting.

Kat looked at him, his nostrils flared as he stared back at her. This game wasn't going to last long at this rate.

With a trembling hand, Kat took the bottle from him and spun. It landed on Kasey. Heat flared in his eyes. Kat licked her lips and pushed herself up on all fours and slowly crawled across the open space to Kase. All three men watched her as she dragged it out, making the distance seem like miles instead of a couple of feet. Kasey's mouth opened as he drew in a deep breath. His cock twitched against his belly.

Kat flicked a glance at Justin, his eyes darkened with lust. "Make it a good one," he told her.

At the challenge in his voice, she raised one eyebrow. He watched her, daring her to rise to the bait. She'd show him.

She kneeled, placing her breasts near eye level with Kasey and slowly wrapped her arms around his neck. "You don't mind if I get comfortable for this, do you?" she asked.

He cleared his throat. "Not at all, darlin'."

She eased her legs on either side of his body so she was straddling him. His hard cock pressed against the seam of her ass. She shifted her hips, making Kasey hiss in a breath. "You okay?" she teased.

"I'm more than okay." His hands gripped her hips as he shifted her to where he wanted her. His erection pressed against her clit.

She looked over at Justin as he crept closer to them. "This what you had in mind?" she asked him

"I don't know. We'll have to see how the kiss plays out." The hungry growl of his voice made her nipples tighten into painful nubs. He looked ready to bend her over and fuck her hard himself.

Turning her attention back to Kasey, she twirled her fingers into the brown hair at the base of his neck. His eyes drifted shut so she dragged her nail along his neck, enjoying the way his muscles quivered like a contented lion as she caressed him.

Kat wiggled her hips, making Kasey groan. "Christ, Kat, quit teasing me and kiss me already," he growled.

She dipped her head toward him and pressed her lips against his. Soft at first. Teasing. Trying to drag it out to torment not only him but Justin and Duncan who had moved in closer to watch.

Kasey had other ideas. His tongue darted out and tangled with hers. He gripped her hips with his big, work-roughened hands and dragged her clit along his shaft. She could feel her moisture coating his cock as she slid.

A hand cupped her left breast, then a different one cupped her right. Lips pressed against her shoulder blade. Hot breath blew across her neck. Good lord, the sensation of three sets of hands caressing her skin, three hot mouths licking and blowing against her sensitive flesh was almost more than she could take.

There was too much sensation. The tequila was fogging her brain. She couldn't think. Breaking the kiss, she panted. Kasey pressed a hand to the middle of her chest and pushed her back, guiding her to lie down with her legs still wrapped around his waist.

"Pass me a condom," he ordered to no one in particular. A second later, Duncan threw him one and Kasey quickly sheathed himself. With the condom in place, he ran his hand down the front of Kat's body. "Now where was I? Oh yeah, I remember."

He shifted so the tip of his cock was in line with her pussy. But instead of fucking her like she'd expected, he dragged the tip through her wet lips. "You're so wet," he groaned.

Justin leaned down and ran his tongue along the edge of her areola, breathing on her nipple until it pulled even tighter, but never quite touching it. She squirmed. Duncan's head bent and he did the same thing to her other breast. Both of them teasing her, never quite giving her what she needed. Her body was on fire.

Kasey spread her open with one hand and with the other he used his dick to tease her clit. She was so wet it slid all around. She wiggled her hips and groaned. God, they were going to tease her to death.

His thick cock lightly made circles around her clit, tormenting her. His cock, so much thicker than his fingers, hit several spots at once. Even when he was moving away, the size made the effects linger.

Justin and Duncan continued to kiss and lick their way around her chest and stomach, never quite touching where she wanted them the most. Desperate, she gripped the back of their heads and forced them where she needed them to go. Justin chuckled against her skin. The sound puffed his breath out, making her skin tingle where it touched.

"I think she's done being teased, boys." Justin laughed.

Duncan and Justin both sucked her nipple into their mouths at the same time.

"Holy shit," she groaned. Her back arched off the floor, driving her farther into their mouths. She didn't want them to ever stop. Kasey's big cock pressed firmly against her clit and pleasure surged through her. The men continued their synchronized assault. Unable to hold back her scream, she moaned as a mind-blowing orgasm ripped through her.

When she came back to earth, three faces grinned at her. She was too satiated to even care that they all looked so smug.

Justin placed a kiss on her lips. She sighed and closed her eyes, sinking into the kiss. When they broke apart, he smiled. "You ready for the rest of that fantasy we talked about?"

She immediately remembered their conversation about Justin fucking her ass while Kasey fucked her and she sucked off Dunc. Kat moaned. God yes, she was ready.

Justin's eyes flared with heat.

He grabbed the box of condoms from the floor. A slow, sensual grin slid across Kasey's face when he saw Justin pull a bottle of lube out of his bag. "You want us both at the same time?" he asked.

"I want all three of you at the same time," she told him.

Duncan groaned beside her. She smiled at him. "I think I owe you a proper blowjob since you got short-changed last time."

His cock flexed, drawing her stare down. Pre-cum dripped from the tip.

Kasey lay down and gripped her hips, drawing her attention back to him. Kat looked down at his cock. He was so much thicker than Justin and Duncan. She couldn't wait to feel him inside her, filling her completely.

She gripped him with her hand and guided him toward her entrance. It took her a moment to adjust to his size as she slowly lowered herself down. When he was fully seated, Justin placed his hands on her hips. "Lean back, darlin'," he murmured and placed a kiss between her shoulder blades.

Kat pressed back. With Kasey's cock inside her, she already felt so full. Could she do this, could she really take both of them? Justin had fucked her in the ass several times over the past few weeks and they both loved it, but would there be room for him in there with Kasey already filling her so completely? She bit her lip.

Kasey cupped her cheek. "It'll work just fine. He'll go slow."

"You're sure? You've done this before?" she asked. Suddenly, the fact that she was just one in a line of women the men had shared didn't seem like such a bad thing. It was reassuring to know they knew what they were doing in this kind of thing.

"Yeah, honey, we've done this before. Trust us, you'll love it. Just relax," Kasey told her.

At the sound of the lube cap flipping open, she tensed. Oh boy. Kasey groaned as she clenched around him. "You really need to relax, Kat," Kasey groaned.

As Justin placed his cock at the entrance to her ass, Duncan bent down and sucked her nipple into his mouth. Kasey's fingers played with her other nipple.

Enjoying the sensations, she pressed back. She felt Justin slowly pushing into her. He felt so big. Her ass burned and she exhaled.

"That's it, Kat, you're doing great," Justin murmured.

Duncan sucked her nipple firmly and her eyes drifted shut. "God, that feels good." There was definitely something to be said for having extra hands and mouths involved to make a woman forget about what she was actually doing.

Justin pushed past the first barrier and the burning eased considerably. She opened her eyes and looked down at Kasey gritting his teeth to hold himself in check. His nostrils flared wide as he dragged in air.

Kat smiled, she wasn't the only one hanging on by a thread. She pushed back against Justin, wanting them all to enjoy the pleasure the moment had to offer.

"I don't want to hurt you," Justin gritted as she pushed back against him.

"You won't," she told him. She wouldn't be here doing this if she didn't trust him. And in that moment, she relaxed fully, allowing Justin to slide completely in.

She'd never felt so full in her life. But full in such a freakin' amazing way. Her ass was on fire, hurting so good, she just wanted him to move, to bring every last nerve ending in her body to life.

Finally, Kasey shifted his hips, pushing deeper as Justin slid out. The men worked in tandem, so she was continually getting fucked.

Duncan's hands threaded into her hair and she opened her eyes to look at him. The heat and passion she saw in his eyes nearly undid her. He looked desperate for her.

"You think you can handle me as well?" he asked.

"Definitely," she murmured.

She grabbed his long, smooth cock with her hand and guided it to her mouth. Closing her eyes, she let the sensations overtake her. Duncan fucked her mouth while Kasey moved in her pussy and Justin fucked her ass. It was exactly as Justin had described and yet it was nothing like she'd imagined. It was so much more. Part of her had thought she might feel a little bit dirty doing this but she didn't. Somehow these three made her feel cherished, being so careful with her as if she were precious and offering them a gift.

Duncan's fingers dug into her hair, Kasey's dug into her thighs and Justin gripped her hips as they all joined together. As the orgasm built inside her, Kat's heart started racing. Her eyes widened in fear. Holy fuck.

Duncan eased his hands in her hair and stroked her head. "Intense, hey?"

Intense? Intense didn't even begin to describe what she was feeling. Her heart felt as if it were going to burst out of her chest. She looked up at him with her mouth full of his cock and nodded.

He stopped moving and paused. "You need us to stop?"

Kasey stroked his hands softly along her arms. Justin placed a kiss against her back, letting her know he was there. Even in the throes of passion, all three men had her interests in mind. If she wanted them to stop, they all would.

Unable to speak, she shook her head. As intense as this all was, she didn't want them to stop.

Duncan smiled. "It's going to blow your mind when you come, honey."

The men started thrusting again. Nimble fingers dipped down and swirled around her clit. She didn't know who they belonged to and she didn't care. As the orgasm built inside her, it didn't scare her this time. Her heart pounded in her chest. As she gasped for breath, Duncan pulled out of her mouth and fisted his cock with his hand.

"I can't hold out much longer," Justin growled behind her.

"Thank fuck," Kasey groaned.

Kat threw her head back and let the orgasm take her over. She screamed out her release. She dimly felt the men finish, but honestly, at this moment she couldn't have cared less if they did. The freakin' Fourth of July fireworks display was tearing through her body at lightning speed. Her arms gave out and she collapsed against Kasey's chest. His muffled "oof" faintly registered in her orgasm-addled brain but there was no way she was moving.

Justin pulled out. Her body was still floating on a euphoric high so it didn't even hurt. He placed a kiss at the small of her back.

Kasey ran his hands up and down her spine. "You okay?" he asked.

When she didn't answer, he pushed the hair off her forehead and tried to peer at her face. "Kat?"

Before she could reply, she heard Justin's chuckle. "Did we kill you?" he asked with a laugh.

"Almost," she mumbled.

She felt herself being carefully pulled out of Kasey's arms, then she was engulfed by Justin. She'd know those arms and that scent anywhere. He kissed her temple. "Rode you a little too hard, did we?"

"Christ," she muttered.

She could feel his body shake with laughter beneath her. "It's not funny," she grumbled.

"Sure it is."

Kat tried to swat him but she didn't have the strength in her limbs to make them do anything.

Justin kissed her head again. "Get some sleep," he told her.

Sleep. Yeah, that sounded good.

Chapter Twelve

T he following morning, Kat's head rested on Justin's shoulder. He knew the moment she woke up, her breathing changed and he could practically hear the gears in her brain kick in. She pushed up on his chest and looked at him, then at the other two men who lay naked on the floor beside her. She chewed her lower lip nervously as if she were unsure of what to do now that things were open in the light of day.

Justin cupped the back of her head and pulled her toward him. He kissed her, pressing his tongue into her mouth. He didn't let up until she melted against him, a loud moan rumbling out of her chest. That's what he wanted. Complete, mindless surrender. He didn't want her thinking about anything but the way her body felt.

"Mmm, now that's worth getting up for," Kasey murmured beside them. Kat broke the kiss and looked at Kasey. Justin rolled her onto her back. He positioned himself on her right side with Kasey on her left. Propping himself up on his arm, he looked down at her. Kasey lazily ran his tongue around her left nipple. Justin glanced up as Duncan moved toward Kat's legs. Justin placed his hand on her thigh and spread her legs open to give Duncan access. Dunc enjoyed eating a woman's pussy almost as much as he did.

At the first swirl of Duncan's tongue on her inner thigh, Kat's breath hitched. She threaded her hand into Justin's hair and pulled him down toward her. When their lips met, Kat's tongue darted out and pressed into his mouth. Their tongues tangled. She made a soft mewing sound and he broke their kiss to see what his friends were doing that she liked so much. He loved seeing her like this—wild, passionate, her eyes glazed over with arousal. She grabbed his head with her hand and pulled his lips back to hers.

Kat's breathing changed, her short little groans and gasps for breath let him know how close she was. He wanted to drive her over the edge. Licking his way down her neck, he swirled her nipple with his tongue, then sucked it firmly inside and her back arched off the bed. "Yes," she hissed.

The distinctive ringing of his phone broke through the panting in the room. Ignoring it, Justin continued to swirl his tongue around Kat's nipple. The ringing stopped, then a moment later it started up again.

Duncan stood from between Kat's legs. A slight twinge of something shifted in Justin's gut as he watched his best friend sheath himself in a condom so he could fuck Kat.

The phone rang again. Needing to get a handle on his emotions, he stood, grabbed his jeans from the floor and pulled the phone from his pants pocket. "Hello."

"Justin, this is total crap. You can't just make decisions that concern the whole ranch without me," his sister's voice shrilled through the phone line. He glanced over at the trio on the bed.

"Now's not a good time," he growled.

"Make time," Denise snarled back.

He heard a loud rattling and what sounded like the old truck shifting gears. "Are you driving?" he asked.

"Yes, you've been ignoring my calls."

Justin groaned. Jesus, that was just what he needed Denise showing up here and finding them all like this. Fuck, that couldn't happen. "I'll call you right back," he barked.

"You'd better," she ordered.

Perfect. Just what he wanted to deal with, his pissed-off sister.

He grabbed his jeans from the floor and stepped into them, not even bothering to do up the fly.

"Justin," Kat groaned. "What's wrong? Where are you going?"

"Nothing, just ranch crap. You guys continue what you're doing and I'll join in when I wrap up this call."

"You sure?" Kat asked.

Sheathed in a condom, Duncan stood poised at the entrance to Kat's pussy. Lines strained Dunc's face as he waited for Justin to give the okay. All three of them looked expectantly at him, should they stop and wait or continue?

His gut clenched at the idea of leaving Kat alone with his friends.

"Yeah, of course," he muttered. His sister had impeccable timing as always. Knowing this conversation was potentially going to get ugly, Justin stepped outside onto the deck.

He dialed Denise back. "So what's the problem?" he demanded the second his sister answered the phone.

"You changed my order at the feed store. Who the hell do you think you are? We are equals in this ranch, Justin. You might be older but that doesn't give you any right to run roughshod over me."

As his sister raged, his attention drifted toward the cabin, the rough grunts and moans coming through the walls. He wanted to get back in there. Needing to placate his sister, he tried, "Sorry."

"Sorry? Sorry? You think that you can just say sorry and all is forgiven? No, not this time. You need to start treating me with respect..." she continued to ramble on.

Finally, after what seemed like a lifetime, she finally stopped her tirade enough to let him speak. "Look, Denise. I get it. I shouldn't just take over. I won't do it again. All right?"

"You better not," she grumbled.

"I'll try. So we good?" He glanced longingly at the door. *Please say yes.*

"Fine, for now. So when are you guys coming back?"

"Not sure, we'll have to see how things go."

"How's Kat doing? She's not pulling her hair and screaming, being trapped with you three?"

He grinned as he heard Kat moaning in the background. "She doesn't seem to be complaining."

"Well, you make sure you keep her happy. This article means a lot for business, so don't mess it up."

He pictured Kat with her legs spread and his face buried as he feasted on her pussy. "I'm definitely keeping her happy, don't worry."

"Eww, you're so gross. I'm hanging up."

Justin chuckled at his sister's disgusted tone. He pocketed his phone. Time to get back to the party inside. He pushed open the door and stopped dead in his tracks.

Kat was spread out on the bed with Kasey fucking her. Duncan's hands gripped Kasey's hips as he plowed into him from behind. The movement of Dunc's body forced Kasey forward, so Duncan was effectively fucking them both.

Jealousy gripped his gut like a fist. He wanted to rip each of the men off his woman and beat the shit out of both of them. It wasn't just Kasey fucking Kat but Duncan was too.

Kat looked over at him, her eyes glazed with arousal, and somehow she still managed to have her brow wrinkled in confusion. Probably wondering why he was halfway across the room still but Justin couldn't seem to move. His feet were glued to the floor. She held out her hand, beckoning him forward.

"Justin, I want you," she pleaded and wiggled her hand to encourage him forward.

Adrenaline surged through him. Jealous rage mixed with the need to mark his territory as his own. He stalked over to her and pushed his jeans down around his ankles. Kat smiled as he shoved his erection in her face. She licked her lips slowly, then ran her tongue along the head of his cock, tasting the bead of pre-cum that rested on the tip.

He didn't want her to tease him. He wanted to fuck her mouth. Claim every part of her, so she wasn't thinking about anyone but him.

He glanced over at his friends, both watching Kat as she slowly slid her mouth down his shaft. Kat opened her mouth and sucked his cock all the way to the back of her throat. Burying his hand in her hair, he thrust his hips toward her face, fucking her mouth. Kat's eyes widened, then warmed as she lightly raked her teeth along the underside of his shaft. Justin hissed.

Damn, she felt good. Her hot, wet mouth held him tightly as she flicked her tongue against his cock. He glanced over at Kasey and Duncan. Kasey's head was thrown back, resting on Duncan's shoulder, as they both plowed into Kat. Duncan bit Kasey's shoulder and Kase grunted, his hips bucked, then his whole body shuddered as his orgasm tore through him. Duncan thrust once more, then he too groaned out his release. With the other two men finished, Kat slid her mouth off Justin's cock. "You happy here or you want to take their place?"

With a growl, Justin glared at his friends to move. The men smiled, then moved away from Kat, leaving the space for him.

He grabbed a condom and quickly shucked it on. Placing the head of his cock at her entrance, he easily slid inside. Her body was hot and wet. The moment he pressed inside fully, Kat moaned and wrapped her legs around his waist. She grabbed his face and pulled him down for a kiss. Their tongues tangled as he thrust, matching the rhythm of his hips with his mouth. He wanted there to be no doubt about who she was fucking. She was his.

Reaching between them, he rubbed his thumb against her clit and Kat's breathing hitched as she broke the kiss. "Oh god, Jus, that feels good."

"It's going to feel a whole lot better in a minute." He ran his tongue along her neck and bit the soft spot at the top of her shoulder that always made her squirm. Her back arched, her pussy spasmed against him. He could feel how close she was. He swirled his finger around the tight bud, then pressed it as he thrust deep and Kat screamed. Her orgasm forced her back off the bed as she arched, her legs clamped around his waist like a vise as she rode out what felt like an incredible orgasm. He continued to thrust into her, the muscles of her pussy clenching and releasing against him, pulling his orgasm from his dick. His balls pulled up tight and with one final thrust she dragged him over the edge. He groaned out his own release, then collapsed against her.

Kat lay limply beneath him on the bed. Finally, she murmured, "I think you guys killed me."

"Yeah, but what a way to go," Duncan's husky voice spoke from his reclined position on the bed beside them.

Justin tensed. He shifted and looked over at his friends. Everything in him wanted to pound the satiated look off their faces. What was the matter with him?

He pushed himself off the bed and shoved his jeans on.

"You okay?" Kat asked him. She raised herself up on her elbow. Concern knit her brow as she studied him.

"I need to go. Denise needs me back at the house."

"Everything okay?" Kasey asked.

"Yeah, it's fine, just some paperwork and stuff," he mumbled. The lie slid easily off his tongue.

Kasey and Duncan exchanged a look, then Dunc said, "If you don't need us, then we're going to hang out, do some more fishing, so we'll see you back at the house later."

Kat scooted off the bed. "Just let me throw my clothes on," she told him.

"You don't have to come with me," he muttered.

"Don't be an idiot, of course I'm coming with you," she scoffed.

Justin felt the slight shift of tension in his gut that she'd chosen to come with him rather than stay. As she stood naked in front of him, he couldn't keep his eyes off her. Even as angry as he was, he wanted her again. Hell, maybe he wanted her because he was angry. Either way, it pissed him off. "Fine, hurry up," he growled.

Kat paused from buttoning up her jeans and looked at him. "You sure everything is all right?"

"Yeah." He grabbed his bag off the floor and slung it over his shoulder. "Later," he called and walked out the door.

Outside, Kat caught up with him as he saddled up the horses. She grabbed his arm and pulled him so he looked at her. Worry lined her face. "What's wrong? Talk to me," she pleaded.

How do you tell a woman whom you are supposed to keep things casual with that you're a jealous prick? This wasn't who he was. Being emotional pissed him off. Being jealous pissed him off even more. He just needed some time to get his head on straight and figure things out. "Nothing, I've just got a lot on my mind," he grumbled.

That excuse allowed them to ride back to the house in silence. As uncomfortable as that was, it was so much better than talking. He could feel her watching him, studying him as she tried to figure him out, but she remained silent. Thank god because he had no idea what he'd say.

Back at the barn, they dismounted. He grabbed the bucket of brushes and looped Scout's reins over the post. Kat grabbed his arm. "Justin."

He looked over at her. Damn it, he wanted to fuck her, stake his claim on her.

"Let me take care of Scout," she told him.

"Why?"

"You've got stuff to do. It's obviously weighing on you. Let me take Scout so you can focus on what you need to."

Looking into her eyes, he saw the blue and gray stormed with emotion, confusion, concern and something else lurked beneath the surface. He should reassure her, let her know everything was all right, but he honestly didn't know if it was.

God, he was a coward. Yeah, he had things on his mind. Her. Them. What a mess. He knew he needed to talk to her but what the hell was he supposed to say? So instead he grumbled, "Thanks." And walked away.

After spending the night alone in her bed, then finding Justin had already headed out to work when she made it to breakfast, Kat was done. Spotting him near the barn, she stormed outside. She'd had enough of this crap.

"What the fuck is your problem?" Kat placed her hands on her hips and stared at Justin. Ever since he'd walked in on her and his friends all fucking he'd been a complete douche. The only reason she'd agreed to the fantasy was because he'd guaranteed her that things wouldn't get messy.

"Nothing," he growled back. "What's yours?"

She rolled her eyes. "Are you seriously going to pretend that nothing is wrong?"

He wouldn't meet her eyes as he looked down at his boots. "Everything's fine."

"Yeah right," she scoffed. "You won't even look at me."

He ran his hands through his hair. "Fine, you want to do this here?" he asked, looking around the paddock. A few hundred feet away several cowboys hoisted bales onto the back of the flatbed.

"Here's as good as anyplace." She wasn't from New York for nothing. She'd be damned if she'd back down just because someone might overhear.

"Fine." He adjusted his hat and pulled the brim down, still not meeting her eyes. "You were right. The whole group thing was a bad idea."

"Are you fucking kidding me?"

"No."

She snorted. "Unbelievable. So it turns out that activity is better with a buckle bunny after all?"

"No, it just turns out you're more of a buckle bunny than I'd thought."

Ouch. "Fuck you," she gritted out between clenched teeth. Turning on her heel, she stormed away from him.

Pain lanced through her chest and she forced herself to keep moving. There was no way she was going to break down in front of all these cowboys.

In hindsight, having the discussion in the open was a bad idea. Jesus, who was she kidding? The conversation would have hurt no matter where they had it. She pushed open the door to the house and raced up the stairs. Slamming her bedroom door, she slumped onto the floor and let the tears fall.

How could she have been such an idiot? She'd honestly believed him when he'd said it wouldn't change things. Fuck, how stupid could she be? Of course, he saw her as a slut. She'd spent the night fucking three men at the same time. She'd known it was a bad idea even when he'd made the offer, but somehow she'd thought the connection between them was strong enough to withstand any uncomfortable morning-after stuff.

Hell, he'd shared women before with those guys. He should have known what that made him think of the women who did that. She wiped a tear from her cheek and laughed mirthlessly. He did know what he thought of those women, he just now thought she was like that too.

She wrapped her arms around her legs and dropped her head onto her knees and let the tears fall. God, how stupid could she be? How many times had she been hit on by professional athletes? She knew what they were like. Knew they weren't worth fucking up her job for but she'd been sucked in by that goddamn cowboy charm. She'd thought Justin was different. Hell, she'd fallen for the loser. Even been spinning around the possibility of seeing if they couldn't possibly continue long distance. That's why she'd tossed out the idea of him coming to New York. What an idiot.

How the hell was she supposed to spend the next three weeks here? When everything reminded her of him, of them? Not only had she lost him but because of her choices she might have ruined her career as well. Would he even be willing to continue on with the interview? What if he sent her packing?

"Jesus," she sobbed. Things couldn't get much worse.

Chapter Thirteen

H ead pounding, she glanced up at the bedside clock. The little red numbers read 10:23 a.m. She'd been sitting here crying for over an hour. Pathetic.

A knock sounded on the door, shaking the wood against her back.

"Kat?" Denise's voice tentatively called through the oak.

She wiped her arm across her eyes and nose and stood. Taking a deep breath, she pulled the door open.

"Hey." Denise smiled sadly. "You okay?"

"Sure," she mumbled and rubbed her hand against her nose again. "Allergies."

Denise tipped her head, a look of understanding passed across her face. "Look, I'm heading to Phoenix to deliver a horse today, why don't you come with me? We'll stay a couple of nights, meet up with some friends of mine and come back on Thursday." Denise squeezed her shoulder. "It'll give you a chance to forget about things with my idiot brother for a little bit.

Kat rubbed her hand across her face. God, how pathetic was she that Denise knew exactly what her problem was? The other woman had warned her, but did she listen? Of course not. She thought she could handle things. Hell, it had made her feel powerful to know three men wanted her. She sure didn't feel powerful now. She felt broken.

"Come on, it'll be great. Besides, you've been here for nearly a month and you haven't had a chance to have any fun."

She'd been having a lot of fun until Justin started acting like an idiot. But maybe getting away for a couple of days was a good idea. Hopefully, when she came back, she'd have a handle on her emotions. The thought of working side by side with him for the next three weeks made her cringe, assuming she still had a job. She'd known it was a bad idea to get involved with him, but she'd been swayed by that cowboy charm and those damn blue eyes. She glanced back at Denise who watched her expectantly.

"Sure, that'd be good, thanks." Happy that Denise and she were still friends, Kat forced herself to smile at the other woman.

"Great. Now pack a bag and let's get out of here."

Justin dropped down onto the porch swing. He slapped his hat against his leg, sending dust flying, then wiped his arm across his forehead. Today had been a bitch. The sound of the screen door opening had him lifting his head. Duncan walked across the porch with two beers in hand.

"Make yourself at home," Justin muttered.

Duncan raised his eyebrow at the belligerent tone. He handed Justin one beer and leaned against the porch railing.

"So what the hell's your problem, man?" Duncan asked.

"Nothing." Justin rubbed his hand across his face. Just what he needed—Duncan wanting to talk.

His friend's snorted laugh made him scowl. "What?"

"I think our definitions of nothing are a bit different there, Jus." Duncan took a pull on his beer. "Okay, so if nothing's going on, then how come you've been such a douche since the other morning?"

Sitting up straighter in his chair, he glared at his friend. "I haven't been a douche."

Duncan raised his eyebrow. "Yeah, you have."

Rubbing the back of his neck, Justin looked everywhere but at his best friend. How the hell did he explain this to him? To avoid meeting Duncan's eyes, he started to peel the damp label off his beer bottle.

"Right, I get it," Dunc snapped. The simple words were laced with so much anger it bit deep into Justin's gut.

"You get what?" Justin growled. How the hell could Dunc get it when he didn't know what the hell his own problem was?

Duncan stared at him, then shook his head sadly. "Look, man, it's cool. I know it's not your thing and honestly it wasn't really fair for us to do that to you."

Justin stopped mid-peel, the bottle lay limp in his hand as he looked at his oldest friend. "What the hell are you talking about?"

"Come on, Jus, I know how it creeps you out that Kase and I fuck."

Where the hell did that come from? He hadn't had a problem with them being together, hell, he'd seen them up close and personal multiple times throughout the weekend. "It doesn't creep me out."

"Yeah right, that's why you haven't been able to look at me all week."

What a mess this had all turned into. He stood and walked to the edge of the porch, looking out across the land that had been in his family for generations. Gripping the handrail, he muttered, "It has nothing to do with you and Kase. Well, not really."

"Right, 'cause watching me pound Kasey's ass while he fucked your girl was cool."

Justin laughed. "Very eloquent, Dunc."

"Fuck that. Come on, man, I'm sorry. I know you're cool with everything between Kase and I in theory but seeing it is a whole other thing."

Rubbing his hand over his eyes, Justin sighed. "Honestly, bro, that has nothing to do with it." He shifted his shoulders, this was really not a conversation he'd ever pictured himself having. "It's not my thing, but seriously it doesn't bother me. I mean, shit, it's not like I didn't know you were touching each other when we were all together, and as long as your hands don't stray to me, why the hell should I care?"

Duncan stared at him. "Then what the hell's your problem?"

"Ugh," he groaned. "I don't know, man. It's not that you and Kasey were together. Hell, I wouldn't have cared if you fucked him while I was there the whole time. Shit," he grunted and rubbed his hand over his head. "It was not being there that fucked me up."

Duncan's brows knit together in confusion.

"I don't know how to explain it. Walking in and seeing you guys with Kat alone, it just kind of fucked me up."

Duncan burst out laughing.

"What's so funny?" Justin growled.

"The big bad Justin Shaw has finally fallen." Duncan grinned like an idiot. "I never thought I'd see the day. And knocked to your knees by a little spitfire, too."

He bristled at the statement and scowled. "I haven't fallen for anything."

"Yeah right, 'cause you get jealous enough to pout like a little girl all the time."

"Fuck you."

"No thanks. I already told you, Kasey's more my taste." Duncan snickered. "So what are you going to do about it?"

Ruin everything, apparently. "Nothing, I ended things."

"Man, you're an even bigger douche than I thought. You can't be serious."

"Dead serious." Justin lifted his bottle to his lips and took a pull of the yeasty brew as he looked out toward the paddock. It was better this way. Duncan was right.

He was acting like a little girl already. Fuck, if this kept up he'd be crying like some pansy ass by the time she left.

"Jus, I've never seen you like this over a woman before. Don't screw that up."

He laughed without humor. "Too late."

Duncan groaned. "What did you do?"

"I, umm...I kind of said she was more of a buckle bunny than I'd expected."

Duncan covered his mouth with his hand. "Oh Jesus, tell me you didn't say that."

He sipped deeply on the bottle, draining the last of the beer, then he set it on the rail. "I did."

Dunc winced. "Damn, you know how she feels about those women."

"I know." He rubbed the back of his neck again, feeling the knots forming beneath his fingers. "It was just..." He paused, trying to find the right way to explain it without sounding like a big sap. "Seeing her with you guys. Knowing she wanted you both without me there, it just..." He exhaled audibly. "I don't know, it pissed me off."

Duncan's hand clasped down on his shoulder. "I get it, buddy. That green-eyed monster is a bitch."

Justin leaned his elbows onto the railing and dropped his head. "It's more than that, though." He shook his head.

Duncan's hand squeezed down. "I know, and for what it's worth, I'm sorry. Honestly, it never occurred to me that you'd care. I mean shit, how many women have we shared? Once you invited us into the room, I figured it was business as usual."

He looked down at the ground as the knowledge sank in. "I know. It shocked the hell out of me, too."

Dunc dropped his arm and started to walk away, then turned back. "So you were cool sharing her when you were in the room but when you weren't it was a deal breaker?"

"Something like that." What kind of perv was he that he'd liked sharing her with his friends? Hell, if he was as crazy about her as it seemed shouldn't that part have bothered him too? What a mess.

Duncan laughed. "Good to know for future reference. Don't fuck Kat unless Justin is in the room."

Without raising his head, Justin growled and flipped Duncan the finger.

"Talk to her, man," Duncan called as he jumped down the front steps and walked toward the bunkhouse.

Justin stood rooted to his spot at the railing as the sun set on the horizon. The pinks and oranges swept across the plains, blanketing the dusty terrain. As the sun dipped behind the Rincon Mountains, Justin was no closer to figuring out what the hell he wanted to do about Kat. But things were far from over. He grabbed his empty beer bottle and made his way inside.

Chapter Fourteen

<hr>

Denise pulled the big dually to a stop in front of the sprawling ranch house. Kat looked up at the wide porch and white picket rails and took a deep breath. God, she was going to miss this place. She'd only been here a few short weeks and already it felt like home. She hadn't realized how restless she'd been in New York. She eyed the porch swing. Memories of her evening make-out sessions with Justin immediately swarmed her senses. She frowned. At least she had her memories, since even those stolen kisses were now a thing of the past.

Pushing open the passenger door, she jumped down from the cab of the truck. She grabbed her bag from behind the seat and slung it over her shoulder. Her head still pounded from the two-day bender they'd gone on.

Rounding the front of the truck, she smiled at Denise. "Thanks for letting me tag along. I had a great time."

"Me too. But, lord, you East Coast girls can tie one on." Placing a hand on her stomach, Denise groaned. "If I never see another Irish car bomb in my life, it will be too soon."

Kat giggled. Yeah, they had drank more than their fair share of those but they were so much better than Dr Pepper, which is what Denise's friends wanted to drink.

"I'll have to come up with something different for next time." The moment the words were out of her mouth, she grimaced. Would there be a next time? How many people hung out with the sisters of their ex? Not many.

She pressed her lips tightly together as a wave of sadness swept through her. Damn it. Why had she let Justin talk her into inviting his friends into the bedroom? Everything had been great until then. Screw that. He'd invited them. If anyone was to blame for how this played out, it was *him*.

As they made their way up the porch steps, the screen door squeaked open and Justin stepped out. He nodded to his sister, then nervously looked at Kat and gave her a slight smile. "Hey, you're back."

"We are," Denise replied. She grabbed Justin's forearm as she walked past and said something too quietly for Kat to hear. Justin smiled weakly in reply.

As Justin talked to his sister, Kat allowed herself the pleasure of drinking in the sight of him. Wow, he looked good. His forearms bunched beneath the rolled-up sleeves of his chambray shirt. His worn jeans wrapped tightly around his powerful thighs as he stepped for-ward.

Raising her face to meet his eyes, she inhaled deeply. He stared back at her, taking in every detail of her face.

Damn him and those piercing blue eyes that seemed to see right into her.

She lowered her stare, not wanting to let him know exactly how hard it was to be near him and not be allowed to touch him.

"Can we talk for a minute?" he asked.

Kat set her bag down on the porch and took a deep breath, steeling herself for the upcoming conversation. Denise had already assured her that as part owner of the ranch she had as much say as Justin in whether Kat stayed or not, so she knew her job was secure but would Justin be okay with her staying?

Justin took her hand and pulled her over to the swing.

Memories crashed over her as she sat down. The way she'd rested her head on his shoulder as they looked across the landscape as dusk fell. The feel of his lips on hers as he coaxed her into surrendering to him. The way his breath felt against her neck mixed in with the night air. Damn. Kat took a deep breath and exhaled slowly, then turned to Justin.

"So what did you want to talk about?" she asked.

Justin raised his head and watched her. "Look, about the umm...the other day." He rubbed the back of his neck and winced. "I was a jerk."

Kat snorted. That was an understatement. "You think?" she scoffed.

The wind blew softly, sending the wind chimes on the corner of the house into song. Kat glanced over and watched the metal flow back and forth.

"Kat, I don't really know what to say about my behavior. Can we maybe blame it on heat stroke?"

God, even now he was making excuses. He probably thought she was going to make things difficult for him for the rest of her stay. Well, she wouldn't, but that didn't mean she had to sit here and listen to him make excuses about why he wanted out.

Kat pushed herself up from the swing and glanced down at Justin. "We done here?"

As she took a step away from him, Justin grabbed her arm. "No, we're not. Sit."

Bristling at the command, she squared her shoulders and stared back at him.

Justin sighed. "Please."

"Fine," Kat grumbled and dropped back onto the seat.

Justin eased his grip from her forearm and slid his hand down to her palm. He looked at their hands, not making eye contact with her as he absently ran his fingertip across her palm, tracing a little pattern. The delicate touch sent a shiver through her body.

Justin took a deep breath and raised his head. "All right, here goes nothing. I'm sorry, Kat. I panicked. I don't really have an excuse, I just..." He exhaled. "When I walked in and saw you with Kasey and Duncan, I was jealous, plain and simple."

Confusion etched across her face. "Jealous, why?"

"What do you mean why? You were fucking them."

"I know but I'd already fucked them both a couple of times with you."

"Yeah. With me."

"What? What's the difference?"

"What do you mean what's the difference? When I walked in, you were fucking them and it really didn't matter to you that I hadn't been there."

Kat spun in her seat to face him directly. "What do you mean it didn't matter to me? Of course it did. Do you think I wouldn't have preferred if you were there? You took off just like you always do in the morning. I was feeling vulnerable and more than a little wigged-out about what happened. Duncan and Kasey knew that and they—"

She paused, looking for the right way to explain what had happened. "They made me feel less ashamed of what we'd done. I don't how to explain this to you properly but somehow having them trust me enough to be *with* them made me realize how special what they have is. It stupidly made me hopeful." Tears welled up behind her eyes and she blinked them back.

"What do you mean hopeful?"

"Nothing. Forget it," she mumbled. Unable to look at him, she glanced back over at the wind chimes happily blowing in the breeze.

"Do you want to be with them?" Justin asked.

She jerked at the question and shot her attention back to him. "What? No, of course not."

"Hopeful about what then?"

She flicked her attention away from him, afraid he would be able to see exactly how she felt about him if she didn't. "Forget it."

"No, I'm not going to forget about it. If being with them like that made you realize you wanted to be with them instead of me, I'm a big boy, I'll handle it. So why don't you just tell me what you were so hopeful about."

"Us, you idiot."

Justin's eyes widened. "Us?" A smile slid across his face. "What do you mean us?"

"I mean us, you and me. Don't get me wrong, I enjoyed being with Duncan and Kasey but it was nothing like when you were with us. Nothing like it is when it's just the two of us. It was sex with them."

"And with me?"

"Come on, Jus, please, haven't I humiliated myself enough here?" She sighed.

He slid closer to her on the seat. "How have you humiliated yourself? I'm the one who got all jealous asshole."

She laughed. "That's true."

He took her hand in his again and looked at her intently. The flecks in his eyes radiated with emotion. "What was different when I was there?"

Kat stared at him, afraid to open up and tell him exactly what she felt for him.

"Come on, Kat, talk to me."

She breathed in deeply and exhaled, then finally looked at him again. "Fine. I don't know, umm...being with them without you felt empty. It was sex for me. For them, it was deeper. Maybe that sounds weird but watching them together was beautiful. And for them, having me there didn't change what they felt for each other. I don't know, I was kind of like a toy they used to enhance what they had, you know?"

Justin nodded. "I think so." He rubbed his hand across his face. "Weirdly enough, I totally get that."

"Really?" God, she hoped so. She'd really enjoyed having Duncan and Kasey join them in bed, but what she'd realized was it was soooo much better when Justin was there, too. Without him, it had felt wrong somehow.

Maybe the fact that he'd gotten so jealous meant he felt it too.

"Yeah, really. Oddly enough, I didn't mind sharing you with them when I was there, but somehow you guys getting together without me kind of freaked me out."

Hope sprang in her chest at the admission. "Why?"

"I got scared you'd want to be with them instead."

She grabbed his thigh with her hand. "Oh my god, no. If anything, I realized how much I needed you there with me."

"Honestly?"

"Yes. God, Justin. I'm crazy about you, you have to know that." She licked her lips. "Hell, I would never have allowed Kasey and Duncan into our bed if I wasn't."

"What?" His brow wrinkled in confusion. "You're going to have to explain that one to me."

"I feel safe with you in a way I never have with anyone else. Safe enough to admit my fantasies. Safe enough to not be ashamed of them. Or at least I did until you called me a buckle bunny."

He winced. "Yeah, about that, I'm sorry. That was completely uncalled for. I was an asshole."

"Yeah, you were."

"I don't really know how to apologize." He paused and made an odd sound, as if it was difficult to get the words to slide across his tongue. "I was jealous and hurt and I lashed out at you. I know it's no excuse but there it is."

Hearing how much the admission cost him helped to ease the pain of what he'd said. She understood more than most how things could be said in the heat of the moment that you wish you could take back. And if he could share his feelings with her, she owed it to him to do the same. "I can't imagine having been willing to try that without you there." She glanced down at her hand on his thigh.

Justin placed his fingers under her chin and forced her to look at him. "Kat, you are safe with me, and I'm glad you trusted me enough to tell me what you wanted."

"But?" she asked when he hesitated.

"But I have to admit, I'm not man enough to stand back and let you go fuck whoever you want without me there."

"You're not man enough?"

He shook his head. "Nope, I can't handle it. I'm cool with us having Kase and Dunc join us again in bed, 'cause I'd be lying if I said that wasn't hotter than hell. But honestly, I'm not cool with you being with them without me."

The hope that had been blossoming in her chest throughout this conversation sprang free and a smile spread across her face. "So what are you saying?"

"I'm saying I fucked up letting you go, and I want to make that right. I want to be the guy you tell your fantasies to. I want to be the person you explore them with."

"Yeah?"

He wrapped his hand around the back of her neck and pulled her head toward him. "Oh yeah," he said against her mouth a moment before his lips crashed down on hers.

"Show me," she whispered and kissed him.

With a groan, he swept her up into his arms and stalked across the deck. He threw open the front door and walked right past an amused Denise, who stood in the kitchen doorway with a huge smile on her face. Kat grinned at the other woman when she gave her two thumbs up.

Justin carried her past the doorway to the guest bedroom and continued down the hall to his room. Taking her there for the first time. He laid her on his bed and followed her down, positioning himself on top of her.

His blue eyes stormed with arousal as he looked at her. His nostrils flared as his eyes raked over her body and she sighed. Damn, she loved when he looked at her like that, as if she were everything he'd ever wanted.

Justin kissed her, softly at first, the kind of kisses that said he could gladly do this all day. *Well, she couldn't.* Kat threaded her fingers through his hair, pressed her tongue into his mouth and ran it along the inside until his tangled with hers.

Strong, sure hands slowly pushed her shirt up as his calloused palms teased across her belly. Her stomach muscles quivered beneath his touch. How was it possible to have missed him so much in just a couple of days? The reverent way he touched her body spoke of how strongly the moment touched him, too.

He pushed her shirt up, baring her breasts. "Damn, Kat," he groaned when he saw the black lace demi-cup bra. The fabric barely covered the tips of her nipples, teasing. By the way his nostrils flared as he looked at her, the little bit of fabric was doing its job.

Justin flicked the bra down, exposing one breast, then the other. He licked his lips, then bent and sucked her nipple into his mouth. Moist heat engulfed the tip and she held his head there. He chuckled and sucked the peak into his mouth, hard, pressing it against the roof of his mouth. Her back arched off the bed of its own volition.

His tongue swirled around her other nipple, then he kissed and licked his way down her body. He trailed his finger around the waistband of her jeans and carefully undid the button.

Anticipation coiled through her stomach. He worshipped her body, paying special attention to each little spot he discovered along the way. Damn it, she just wanted him to hurry already. This slow, torturous teasing was driving her crazy. She was so wet, with one little flick on her clit she would come undone. Her entire body trembled with need. She lifted her hips to encourage him to touch her.

He chuckled again. "Patience, darlin'," he said. He rubbed the heel of his hand against the seam of her jeans, pressing the firm fabric against her clit. Her entire body shuddered.

"Yes," she hissed. That was exactly what she needed.

"Fuck, I can't wait," he growled. The slow, calm tormentor was gone. In its place was the wild, hungry man she had come to love. Her jeans hit the floor, followed by her panties.

"Oh sweetheart," he groaned as he reverently looked at her pussy. He ran his finger along her labia. "You're enough to torment a saint," he uttered.

Justin positioned his shoulders between her legs. He wrapped his hands under her ass and brought her up to his mouth. He inhaled deeply. "Jesus, I missed you," he growled, then swept his tongue along her pussy.

He swirled around her clit. Exhaling, he blew a puff of air against the sensitive flesh. The combination of his hot, wet tongue mixed with the puff and holy cow it felt amazing. She widened her legs, needing to feel more of him.

Threading her hands through his hair, she held him in place. This time, he allowed her to hold him there. His finger slid inside her, fucking her as his tongue slurped at her clit.

"Don't stop, Jus," she moaned.

He lightly nibbled her clit with his lips and the slight edge of teeth. A shudder ran through her. Looking up, he met her stare and held it as he ran his other hand through her wet pussy, then trailed his finger down to her ass. She shifted against the mattress.

He grinned and sucked her clit into his mouth. With his one hand teasing her ass and the other fucking her pussy, Kat's body was on overload. All of her senses fired to life.

His finger slid inside her ass at the same time he sucked hard on her clit and the combination sent her tumbling toward orgasm. She clamped her thighs tightly against his head, holding him in place, not wanting the orgasm to ever end.

When she came back down to earth, Justin smiled at her. Somewhere along the line he'd ditched his jeans and knelt in front of her, his erection throbbed beneath her stare.

"I want you, Jus," she told him.

He ripped into the condom wrapper with his teeth and within seconds, he was sheathed and poised at her entrance. His hard cock flexed at the entrance to her pussy. She gripped his tight ass in her hands and pulled him toward her.

"I want you inside me," she demanded.

He slowly pushed inside. When he was fully seated, she sighed, enjoying the full feeling. His jaw flexed tight as he held himself still. The effort not to move obviously cost him as his dick twitched inside.

Digging her heels into his ass, she arched her hips. He eased back and slowly slid forward again. The slow movement dragged out the sensual torture, hitting every nerve ending along the way.

She slapped his butt.

"Move your ass, cowboy."

Justin growled but did as she requested. He pulled back and thrust forward. Slowly, drawing it out. When he was fully sheathed inside, he paused and held still. Showing her a tenderness he'd never shown her before. In the past, it had always been hard and fast, a pounding rhythm they both enjoyed. Kat clenched her internal muscles around him and he groaned. "Do that again," he commanded.

Kat flexed again, the action triggering something inside her. He swiveled his hips. Her pussy clenched around him as he hit her G-spot. Damn, that felt freakin' amazing. Justin rubbed her clit at the same time he thrust forward. Her breathing hitched as her orgasm drew near.

"Look at me, Kat."

She forced her eyes opened and watched him. The cords in his neck stood out, his nostrils flared as he moved. He looked so sexy.

Their eyes locked and held. He thrust and swiveled again and again. She felt completely connected to him, as if he was allowing her to see a part of himself he'd never shown anyone before, something she'd never shown anyone either. That realization tore through her, making the orgasm that dragged along in its wake more intense than anything she'd ever felt.

As her pussy spasmed and her orgasm gripped her, Justin groaned above her, shuddering with his own orgasm.

He dipped his head and pressed his lips to hers. Their tongues tangled. She put everything she was feeling into the kiss.

How was it possible to feel so strongly about someone in only a matter of weeks? After what they'd just experienced together, she had no doubt he felt the same way about her.

Justin pushed himself up onto his elbows. His hand traced the line of her face as he looked down at her. "You don't know how many times I've pictured you here in my bed."

She smiled. "Then why didn't we ever come in here before?" she asked.

"Because I didn't want to remember being in here with you when you were gone," he told her.

Kat's heart flipped at the honest admission ripped from her strong cowboy. "And now?"

"And now I need you here, in my bed where you belong. We'll figure out the rest later." He bent and softly pressed his lips against hers. The tenderness in the kiss undid her.

Definitely later, she thought as she sank into his kiss.

THE END

****For upcoming releases, exclusive content, contests and giveaways, be sure to Subscribe to my newsletter**

Plus as a newsletter subscriber you'll get access to a newsletter subscriber-only FREE book.

**Want a sneak peak at Book 2 in the Cowboy Code Series, Rough Stock, keep swiping.

Excerpt Rough Stock- Book 2 Cowboy Code Series

T he Thunderhead Ranch sign loomed in front of him as Brody Kyle turned his truck off the highway onto the winding road that would lead him to his destination. He tapped his fingers on the steering wheel along to the beat of the death metal song pounding through the stereo. Since he was a cowboy, everyone assumed he'd be into country music and line dancing, and he was when it impressed the ladies, but given the choice he'd take the hard, driving beat of metal any day.

Even with the stereo cranked, he still couldn't drown out his thoughts. What if she said no? His nerves twisted in his gut. This had to work.

After his horse had fallen during the final trials of the season and shattered his leg, Brody knew his only chance at success on the tour this year would be to convince Denise Shaw to work with him and his new horse. Without her, his horse would never be ready in time. And he needed to compete in as many events as he could to stand the best chance. There was no way he would get the buckle if he only managed to hit the end of the season.

He'd been dreaming big for so long he could practically taste the victory, the weight of the gold buckle in his hand and how being the champion would feel. Not only to show everyone who said he'd never amount to anything that they were wrong, but to be able to afford to have something real that was his and could never be taken from him. He'd do whatever it took to make that a reality.

Brody could almost picture the ranch he planned to buy. But without competing on the tour, he'd never have enough money in the bank to comfortably own his own spread free and clear. Sure, he could afford something now, but getting it up and running and maintaining it was a whole other issue.

No, he needed at least another season or two of winning to have enough in the bank to carry him through. And without Denise that wasn't going to happen.

The only problem was Denise wasn't like other women. She seemed hell bent on ignoring the attraction between them. Which wasn't going to work in his favor.

He'd been trying to wrangle a date with her for two years, ever since he'd first laid eyes on her. But she wanted no part of it. Hopefully, she wouldn't let that stand in the way of her helping him.

After several minutes, the Shaw homestead came into view. The rambling ranch house with the wide porch was the kind of home Brody had always dreamed of as a kid. Instead, he'd grown up in a ramshackle trailer, which shook every time the wind blew. Unfortunately, the trailer he'd grown up in had been in better shape than his family's ranch, which was probably why the bank had repossessed the property. Losing their home had been the beginning of the end for his family.

In the circular drive, Brody pulled his truck to a stop and jumped down from the cab. He scanned the area around the house, wondering which way he should go in order to find Denise. The barn was probably his best bet.

Before he'd taken more than a half-dozen steps, a lean figure exited the barn. Brody grinned when he saw Duncan.

"Hey," he called out.

A smile spread across Duncan's face. Brody walked toward the other man and the two met somewhere in the middle.

"Hey, man, what are you doing here?" Duncan asked.

"I'm here to see Denise."

In an instant, the friendly smile left his face. "Why do you want to see her?"

What the hell? Was there something going on between Denise and Duncan that he wasn't aware of? He hoped not.

"I want to talk to her about training my new horse."

Duncan's posture relaxed instantly. "Yeah, sorry, man. I heard about Buster taking that fall. You okay?"

Brody's chest gripped tight, squeezing his heart. He'd lost not only his chance at winning but he'd lost a part of himself that day. So, no, he wasn't okay.

Putting Buster down had been like killing his best friend. But how did you admit that to someone, even another cowboy, without sounding like a total wuss? It was his horse, not a family member, despite how much it felt like it. He clenched his jaw tightly. Damn, he hated feeling like this.

Instead of admitting it, he shrugged. "Knee took a bit of a beating, but overall I'm fine." He glanced toward the corral where he assumed Denise worked with the horses. "If Denise can turn my new horse into half the roper Buster was I'll be good and make a run for it again this year."

Duncan clasped a hand on Brody's shoulder and gave it a quick squeeze in a show of support.

Crap, so much for not looking like a wuss.

"If anybody can get your horse ready it's Dee." Duncan glanced over Brody's shoulder toward the truck. "You got him in the back?"

"Yeah, figured Denise wouldn't know if she was willing unless she had a look first."

Duncan snorted. "There isn't a horse around that Dee can't work with. No one's got her touch." A smile spread across Duncan's face as if he was remembering how her touch felt. Brody's knuckles flexed into a fist at the idea of the other man touching the woman he'd wanted for so long.

This was going to be fucking unbearable if Denise and Duncan were an item. He exhaled hard. Somehow, he'd have to handle it. Without Denise's help, he didn't stand a chance of winning all-around cowboy next year.

He needed those cash prizes. And without the winnings, there'd be no huge endorsements, which meant he'd be dragging tail for several more years to earn the money he needed to buy his own place outright. He'd been so close this year until Buster got hurt and everything fell to shit.

Brody looked around the yard again. Where was she? "Is Denise around?"

Duncan laughed. "Yeah, she went in to grab a shower."

"In the middle of the day?"

Duncan snorted. "It was umm...kind of a necessity. Come on, I'll take you inside."

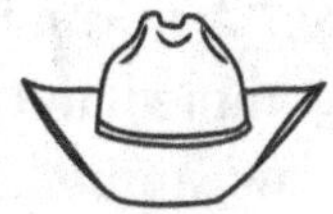

Denise pushed the glass shower door open and pulled a plush, pale-blue towel off the warmer. She wrapped it around her body, then pulled the smaller towel off the rack and twisted it around her hair.

"You need me to wash your back, darlin'?" Duncan's rumbling voice bellowed down the hallway.

Her head snapped up at the sound of his amused voice. She snarled, remembering the way he'd laughed himself silly while she lay covered in manure after slipping on the ground. Next time she'd step on the damn dog's tail and be done with it. "If you come anywhere near me, Duncan Kane, you won't be able to sit on your horse for a month, let alone do anything else."

The jerk hadn't even given her a hand up. Finally, he'd held out the end of his shovel for her to grab on to so he could pull her up since he didn't want to touch her. Not that she could blame him, but that was beside the point.

"Come on, it can't be any worse than some of those potions you're always putting on your face. Don't some of those have bat dung in 'em? What's the difference?" Duncan asked.

Oh, he was going to pay. She stormed out of the bathroom, wielding her hair brush to whack him. As she rounded the corner, she stopped dead in her tracks. Holy shit, Brody Kyle. Her hand immediately went to her hair and she ripped the towel turban off her head.

She closed her eyes and groaned. Oh god, could this get more embarrassing? A normal person would have covered themselves up immediately, but no, not her, she instantly thought of how stupid she must look with a fuzzy, pink-cheetah-print towel on her head. This was mortifying.

"Hi, Denise." Brody's whiskey-roughened voice glided over her skin like a caress. What was it about him that immediately turned her into a bumbling *girl*? She was a strong woman who could hold her own with any man on the ranch but within seconds of being around Brody Kyle she was a giggly twit who couldn't control herself. Probably why she usually avoided him like the plague. Well, that and his "love 'em and leave 'em" reputation.

She pressed the towel against her chest. The last thing she needed was for it to fall. That would just be the icing on the humiliation cake.

"You sure I can't dry your back, Dee?" Duncan teased. She opened her eyes and looked at him. He grinned and waggled his eyebrows ridiculously at her. How could she stay mad at him?

She laughed. "No, you big loser, you can't dry my back. If you want to be helpful, go clean up the shit."

Duncan shrugged. "Ah well, can't blame a guy for trying." He turned halfway around, then touched his finger to his cheek. "Ah, Dee, you missed a spot."

Oh my god, no. Her hands flew to her face and the offending mark. The second she let go of her towel, it fell to the floor. With a squeal, she grabbed it, clasped it in front of her and tore off down the hall, knowing full well her ass was completely on display. Better her ass than her front.

She slammed the bedroom door and flopped onto her bed, completely mortified. Brody Kyle had seen her run buck-ass naked out of a room. *Just shoot me now.* Not only that, but Duncan had witnessed the whole thing. She'd never live this down. *Oh god, please don't let my ass have been jiggly*

Denise sat up and looked at herself in the mirror. Her face was a flaming red but other than that it was clean. Son of a bitch. "I'm going to kill you, Duncan," she yelled.

His chuckling reply drifted through the closed door. "It was worth it, darlin'. I'm heading back out. Brody will be in the kitchen waiting for you, so don't take too long."

She flopped onto her bed again. No, no, no, she did not want to have to face Brody again today. This day sucked!

Buy Link

About Author

Lauren Fraser resides in British Columbia, Canada, with her husband, two children, and two dogs. When she's not busy writing, Lauren loves to spend time with her family outside—camping, hiking and paddle boarding.

Lauren writes about love and relationships in many different forms, but in the end, she's a sucker for a happy ending. She is multi-published and loves to hear from her readers. For the latest updates, visit her website.

Website http://www.laurenfraser.com/
Newsletter: http://www.laurenfraser.com/newsletter

*If you enjoyed this book please consider leaving an honest review

Also By

Letting Go

The Geek Next Door

Dani's Duo

Longing for Kayla

Too Hot

Sex, Sin and Surf

Aged to Perfection

Yielding for Him

www.ingramcontent.com/pod-product-compliance
Lightning Source LLC
Chambersburg PA
CBHW011037190726

48290CB00011B/2888